UNTITLED...

Publishing-in-support-of,

EDUCREATION PUBLISHING

RZ 94, Sector - 6, Dwarka, New Delhi - 110075
Shubham Vihar, Mangla, Bilaspur, Chhattisgarh - 495001

Website: *www.educreation.in*

ISBN: 978-93-85247-51-4

Price: ₹ 319.00

Printed in India

UNTITLED

Every life needs a Name

Manik Nath
&
Ashish Malviya

EDUCREATION PUBLISHING
(Since 2011)
www.educreation.in

About The Book

Written in backdrop of years to 1998 to 2009, a twenty first century story about two best friends and their simple love stories; A tale of friendship, love and life.

Aayush aka Pappi and Anupam for whom life is about following their heart; Bunking classes, movies, hanging out in woods, picnics by the banks of river Betwa.

They fall in love with two simple yet beautiful girls and start acting foolish. One day impatient Pappi proposes Rinki on the road while she was going to the bus stop for school. Rinki is scared. She denies and runs away. Pappi is heartbroken. That evening he is at the receiving end from both the mothers. Now he has to achieve something in life to get his love.

Anupam wants to get into Abhishikta's good books before proposing her. Once he is advised by one of his friends Shekar to puncture Abhishikta's scooter outside the coaching class and then help her. This way he would get to spend half a day with her. But Anupam runs out of luck and some other guy gets the chance.

As the story unveils hard truths of life and hilarious stupidity of teenagers, the question remains will the two boys get the love of their life.

About The Author

Manik Nath was born in Bhopal, Madhya Pradesh. He completed a degree in engineering and advanced construction management. His previous work experience includes some of the big names of engineering and construction industry in project management functions. He currently lives in Bangalore with his wife and works for a multinational software giant. UNTITLED is his first honest attempt to be an author. He can be reached on facebook or email at:-
manik_nath@yahoo.com.

Ashish Malviya was born in Bhopal, Madhya Pradesh. He graduated from Indore with a degree in Computer science engineering. He has worked in past with some big software multinationals. He currently lives in Pune with his wife and daughter and works for a big multinational bank with the bank's software development division. UNTITLED is his first honest attempt to be an author. He can be reached at facebook or by email at:-
malviya.ashish@gmail.com.

Prologue

Vancouver, Canada 1st July 2007

Orkut Scrapbook of Aayush, scrap from Anupam his best friend: "I woke up to a dream. A dream which has been haunting me since last one year: a dream in which I just keep falling through a dark tube neither dead nor alive. What do I do bro?"

Manchester, UK 1st July 2007

My Scrapbook scrap from Aayush: "I know *kaakey* (friend) ever since she is gone from your life you have been getting this dream. But how long mate, tell me how long, it's been more than a year now. Get over it."

Anupam: "Could you ever get over with Rinki. Did you forget her when your love life went haywire?"

Aayush: "No I could never"

Anupam: "Then how do you expect me to forget those 10 years of my life. Those 10 years of life which I loved and dreamt only of Abhishikta. You know what? I went to bungee jumping yesterday with my colleagues here, everybody enjoyed and I laughed, but deep in my heart I was crying; crying for my life, crying for my love, that never reached its epitome. Abhishikta my first love; she left me alone in a dying situation and I cried. I felt like I was going to die falling off the cliff but the moment I got the jerk of the rope tied to me I got the feeling, I'm alive. Alive to get haunted with those memories"

Aayush: "I can feel what you are going through, but you need to get over it. I am there for you if you need anything."

Anupam: "Yes I know that you have been through the thick and thin of my life and always been there with me. You remember those days of school when we used to be so much trouble and every time you have been with me whenever I have called upon a trouble...gosh those were the days..."

This was my conversation on Orkut with my best friend Aayush Kumar aka *Pappi* with whom I shared a friendship of 35 years and a family of the same number of years as well. It was after both of us left India within a gap of 15 days.

35 years of friendship of which almost 10 years of friendship was something which we got in as *viraasat* (inherited) from our fathers who had been friends since their first day of joining at *BHEL, Bhopal or Bharat Heavy Electricals Limited, Bhopal* and to it add 26 years of our age since the day we were born.

Pappi, he is a Computer engineer and I, Anupam, am a Civil engineer. Whenever I think of it; it seems like our lives are tied to some common stuff all the time. When I say common I mean things like, both are engineers of a branch starting with the Alphabet "C", heaven save those Softwares coded by him and those Structures constructed by me: again both products starting with the alphabet comes as "S", and till date both our lives in the last 26 years have incidents which can be called UNTITLED.

The moment I decided to write this novel, thinking of the past 10 years of my life; all my typing on the QWERTY keyboard just made up only one word *'ABHISHIKTA'* , all the 26 alphabets made up only one word *'ABHISHIKTA'* all keys on the keyboard typed out only one name *'ABHISHIKTA'*. The title of my life, which I never got, and life remained **UNTITLED**.

1

SUMMER OF '97

It was 5.00 in the morning in the month of June when ma called me up *"Baba dakh Aayush er phone"* (Son, Aayush has called). I wondered why the hell this guy makes an entry at wrong time.

"Haan Bol" (Yes speak up) I said picking up the receiver frustrated and sleepy,

"What are you doing?"

"I was with Rekha."

"But you are at your home, aren't you?" came the question with a surprised and loud exclamation for an early morning talk.

"Yes you dumb I am at home, sleeping and dreaming about her, what else do you expect from me at 5.00 A.M in the morning?"

"Stop dreaming about her you fool and reach the grounds we have a football match, remember?"

"Don't worry I will be at the grounds." I hated to part ways with Rekha but football was something I was in love with so had to. Hey by the way this didn't mean that I was in love with Rekha.

Rekha of my dreams that morning was not the Bollywood film actress; instead she was a girl in my coaching.

Rekha had joined the coaching institute a week after I joined. She used to come for the early morning classes, but after few days she switched to evening classes which I used to attend. I guess that waking up for Mathematics and physics classes at 5.30 in the morning was a bit too much of torture for that beautiful girl. The day she came and I saw her for the first time it was *"Crush at first sight."* Well I invented this phrase as at that tender age crushes keep happening.

Lost in those thoughts I reached the football grounds, after running a full two kilometres. I was gasping for a few atoms of O_2 when something hit me on the back; I turned around, Pappi was smiling with the Adidas ball in his hand.

Aayush nicknamed Pappi. Nice pet name for a boy huh! I always thought what would have happened if he had this name in his School register.

He loved this name. Whenever I called him by this name in our class all the girls turned around and giggled, this made him feel special. Well feeling special with a name that means kiss in Hindi is quite explainable. At 5'11" he was quite fair by Indian standards, with added good looks and always thought of himself as a movie star. On the other hand I was a lean stick like creature standing at 6'2" with wheatish complexion and not so good looking features. Just the average Indian boy.

"Hey you already up with that falling attire of yours," I asked as I started to take off my tracksuit.

"Why do you keep calling names for my gear?"

"Well that's what you keep doing all the time on the ground. You fall and dive more than the goal-keeper as if that's your favourite sleeping couch." I laughed.

"Shut up. You do not know what football is, until you fall on the ground there is no glory and no one believes that you have skills."

"My Ass!"

"Tell me about Rekha" Pappi asked with a strange desire in his eyes.

"A beautiful actress from the 80s don't you know, she is even said to have had an affair with the superstar Amitabh Bachhan. I thought you knew it, you are a *filmi* freak dude."

"Don't act smart. Tell me about that new girl in coaching about whom you were dreaming in the bed."

"Why do you want to know? I don't like that look in your eyes you pervert. By the way didn't you know, asking anyone a personal question is bad manners!" I said trying to ignore the matter.

"Manners my ass, when was the last time you followed manners huh! Now no more *natak* (drama) and tell me."

"There is nothing to tell."

"Huh! Then why were you dreaming about her?"

"Is there any problem if I dream about her? Are you interested in her?"

"No. But still tell me naa?"

"Arre it's just a crush at first sight kind of thing."

"Are you sure?"

"Yes I'm sure and don't you know that every beautiful girl has a boyfriend and more beautiful a girl is the more chances of her having a boyfriend. I'm not that lucky to be the boyfriend of such a beautiful girl."

"Yeah so very true, I agree. Let's go the match will start in a few minutes."

We reached bench where all players had surrounded Lampat our coach for the briefing before the match; he gave us a warm smile and directed us to take our seats at the bench. He declared the playing formation. It was a typical formation of 4-4-2.

The game was evenly balanced when all of a sudden, the opposition stormed into an attack their main striker who had been in the mid-field came into our penalty box. As the left forward made a beautiful cross our goalie came out like a thunderbolt and leaped at the ball for a hard punch, he managed to get the ball out of danger but in the process he ended up landing one solid knock at the nose of the striker of opposition, seconds later the guy lay down on the ground with his nose spurting out red fluid. The referee took out the yellow card and signalled a penalty against us. We positioned ourselves outside the box while the opposition skipper came to take the shot. Like all good skippers he shot the ball right at the net. We were down by 1-0. First half finished.

Second half started, I took a few free kicks, but everyone is not David Beckham or Christiano Ronaldo and I felt as if my luck had run out for that match. Then came another counter attack and this time our defence came into action. It was very defiantly led by Pappi who as per habit of rolling to the ground did a fabulous sliding tackle relieving the already booked goalie but in the process he hurt his left ankle and laid there groaning in pain. His ankle became double the normal size. He was given immediate treatment by the doctor on the ground and made to sit on the bench.

We entered the 80th minute of the game I got a good pass from our right back. I carried it close to the box and kicked it in air; our skipper flew in air and with a header equalled the scores. We finished having a one all draw.

After the game I took Pappi to hospital. The doctor asked for an x-ray. After the x-ray, the doctor gave Pappi a painkiller injection and asked us to leave and return next day for the report.

Pappi's mom was cutting and peeling the vegetables for lunch, I touched her feet "*Namaste auntyji*," she placed a motherly hand on my head giving her blessing said *"Jeetey Raho beta"* (may you live long). Pappi entered limping as Aunty saw him she hit the roof "ohh what happened to my son? What have you done to yourself? Is everything alright?" Pappi assured her everything is fine. She said "Why do you play such an ugly, insane and *junglee* game? See what has happened."

"Ma its okay I'll be fine."

"Shut up, do not move."

She asked me, "did anything happen to you too beta?"

"No Aunty I am fine." Pappi moved a bit to keep the leg up on table.

Aunty said, "Do not move. I will get some *Haldi* (turmeric) Milk for you."

She went into the kitchen cursing the game of football.

After Pappi drank the *Haldi* Milk, I helped him move to his room and went to say bye to Aunty.

She said, "*Beta* have lunch and then go."

"Aunty, mom must have cooked for me."

"*Beta* (son) either you eat here or there it's the same thing."

"Yes auntyji it's the same thing but that food will get wasted."

"Don't worry your mom will keep it in fridge."

"Ok auntyji but I must inform her."

"Don't worry I will call her up and tell her you go and sit with Pappi, also I need to talk to her it's been days I haven't spoken to her." It felt that I was a son of two families having two lovely and caring mothers.

Later that afternoon when a girl crossed Pappi's house, silently she looked at Pappi, smiled and then walked away. Pappi went head over heels and almost fell off the chair.

I rushed in, he was grinning.

I asked him "Now you tell me what that was?"

"What was what?"

"Now you don't be too smart. I didn't miss any of that smile exchange."

"*Kuch nahi yaar* (nothing my friend), she is just a girl from the neighbourhood."

"Aha! So all girls of your neighbourhood give you a blushing smile when they pass by you or your home. Looks like we have our own SRK (Shahrukh Khan, a popular Bollywood actor) here huh!"

"Yes of course people living in same neighbourhood do such friendly gestures. She is Rinki." His face turned full pink now.

"Look dude you can't hide your feelings from me, so tell me what is it that I know don't? Rinki! That ghost girl of your neighbourhood. She looks so different, I saw her almost a year ago and now she has changed a lot."

"Yes buddy she is the same girl and I happen to like her, that is it."

“Just like her and no love shove business?”

“No, *yaar* no other business. Actually my liking for her is gradually developing.” The word *developing* sounded like as if some sort of life form is *developing* in some test tube or beaker in some remote bio-tech research laboratory in some remote corner of this planet.

I asked him, “When did this strong liking start to develop?”

He grinned “I liked her since my childhood, but recently it has grown pretty strong in the last one year.”

“Hmm by the way where does she live? Has she changed her route just to see you before she goes to her place?”

“She stays down the street just few houses after mine.”

“Aha! Now I understand it’s a very strong connection.”

“Don’t tease me like that.”

“Okay Mr. Pappi but whenever you decide to propose her, give me the news first.”

Next morning the doctor mentioned that although there was no fracture but Pappi had got his ligament injured during the game and was advised full bed rest for next two days, thereafter he can resume normal walking but no sports for the next 1 month.

In the evening I went to his home and I said, "*Kaakey* Raman's admission results are due to be announced."

"Yes mate I know that and hope that we get through." Both of us were changing our schools after our 10th board exams and moving from a missionary School named *St. Xavier's Higher Secondary School* to a School of BHEL Education Society named *Raman Higher Secondary School.* The major reason for this transfer was that now in 11th standard with Mathematics and Science as our main subjects, and the pressure of coaching and *MPPET* or *Madhya Pradesh Pre Engineering Test* mounting on us we had to find out a way of skipping School and study for our competitive exams. Personally I have always felt that these entrance exams are a way to torture kids and their life is being tormented through these entrance exams.

Pappi said, "Don't worry they have a BHEL employees quota of admissions to be given every year and we have a fairly good score in 10th board to get a seat."

We both scored distinction in Mathematics and Science in our 10th board exams and the BHEL quota should have been enough to see us through the admission process. I said, “Yes and I hope that once we get admission in *Raman* we will even clear the *MPPET* exam.”

“I have heard that they let guys slip out of the School by jumping the walls of the School. Won’t it be fun? Once out of the School you will get enough time for everything even studying.”

Soon our commando training was to begin at Raman Higher Secondary School where instead of studying we would be getting trained in jumping over high walls. Could not help thinking that if by some luck I clear the NDA exam, then at least in the defence forces I won’t have to do a lot for wall jumping exercises.

Pappi said, “Dude lets go out for a while, I’m bored with this bed rest.”

“No way man, if Aunty gets a hint she is going to kill me. You better stay where you are and don’t try your smart ideas.” He smiled at me and it was one of those smiles; the typical looks which say that he has some great idea blinking in his genius mind which has at least 95% probability that we both will get killed in action for doing that act. But me being an emotional fool had to hear it. “What?”

Pappi told me that his mom had gone for a *puja* (Hindu prayers) and she won’t be returning for sometime. I heard the *Doordarshan* (state owned television channel of India) news volume and said,

"But your Dad is at home and he won't let us go out."

"Don't worry I will talk to him."

He shouted, "Dad can I go out with Anupam to the local bookshop to get a physics book." He gave us the permission, but with the instruction that we ride carefully.

"Okay dude so you have got everything chalked out for this mission."

As we got out I helped Pappi load his body on to the rear carrier of my bi-cycle. I started to pedal, Pappi shouted, "*Arre* not that way the other way."

"But that's our usual route?"

"Yes but its Friday and Rinki must in temple." I realized that it was not just some mission it was a planned *Black Cat Suicidal Mission*. We were destined to get killed and not even get a *Paramveer Chakra* (India's highest gallantry award) for our gallant efforts. Pappi said, "*Yaar* you have to take risks in love."

"Hey but you said that your love is not confirmed."

"Dude this mission, it's a reconnaissance mission to find out whether there exists true love in my heart or not."

"Fine I do this life threatening mission but you are going to treat me with *samosas* at *choubey's chat* joint, plus *WILLS NAVY CUT* (Indian cigarette brand) will be sponsored by you."

We reached the temple where Rinki was playing *langdi pakad* (game played by Indian kids with one leg folded and trying to chase and catch other kids) with her friends. I recognized a girl whom I had seen quite often in Pappi's neighbourhood and I really didn't like that girl, her name was Bindu. I don't know why but I somehow felt that she had behaviour as 'Don't give me that attitude I have my own' and I hated that. To add to it she had the name of one of India's most famous all time vamp in Bollywood movies.

Rinki saw Pappi seated maharaja style on my bi-cycle with me pedalling laboriously carrying the Prince of heart. We established clear visual id with soft target and Pappi engaged her with his eyes and they had exchanged a few rounds of smiles between them.

Pappi said, "Slow down *yaar* don't be in a hurry."

"Aye Aye Sir" Meanwhile Bindu and rest of Rinki's gang became interested in Pappi.

"Now Sir can we get out of the action zone before we get ourselves killed amidst action."

"*Ya Ya* move mate." Finally, we got out of the combat zone, I was relieved. We headed straight for our *WILLS NAVY CUT* routine of the day.

After having our daily samosas at choubey's chat we moved out and our highly dangerous and risky *Black Cat bi-cycle operation* met its gallant moment. We encountered Pappi's next door neighbour Aunty. The moment we saw her I pedalled at super-sonic speed to lose her off our tail. As soon as we reached home, Pappi's mother entered with the lady with whom we saw and it seemed that we were hit by the Air-to-Air missile named tattle of which was filled with gossip, with some added chemical forms of blab, on which the *mohalla* aunties seemed to have done a PhD.

Neighbour aunty said, *"Arre beta what happened?* Why are you limping? Is everything okay? I just saw both of you at the Choubey's Chaat joint everything looked fine then."

Pappi's mom hearing this shouted, "What? Both of you went out despite of my warning. *Bhabhiji* (sister in law, Indians call neighbours brothers and their wives as sister in laws, we know how to make relations, easy) these guys don't listen to their mother these days. Look he hurt himself at that stupid game of football and now he doesn't rest and keeps moving here and there." Now what started was the routine cribbing of women regarding today's generation, disrespect towards parents and then moved on to discuss the usual neighbourhood gossips. We slowly escaped and went to Pappi's room where I thanked him for this brilliant gallantry award we just received. He said, *"Dost* (friend) let my love story be a success then even your name will be written in golden alphabets."

"No boss sorry I am not interested in golden alphabets."

"Ok see you later and remember our admission results will be out by next week."

2

PAPPI AKA AAYUSH KUMAR - PART 1

I, Aayush Kumar or Pappi after that Orkut chat with my best friend sat down in my hotel room in Canada and stared out of the window as memories of those golden days grasped me.

This replicates introduction given by SRK in *Veer-Zara* (A Bollywood movie starring SRK), but I preferred this introduction as my best friend Anupam has always teased me lovingly as the SRK who couldn't make his way to the Bollywood and ended being a software engineer.

As I looked out of the window it was raining heavily I wished that if by some miracle golden days could come back when I was with my best friend Anupam and my dream girl. My dream girl Rinki Sehgal who lived in my neighbourhood and I loved her since my teenage.

Slowly I went into a world of memories and dreams.

Dreams.....dreams of a Prince with a princess....

Cricket match in neighbourhood, 9 runs needed of the last over I was at the crease and we managed to take 4 runs of the 5 balls, 5 runs needed of the last ball, I was facing the last ball trying to concentrate as a four would lead us to a draw and six will win us the match. Last ball came to me like a rocket, I swung my bat and as Shahrukh Khan never misses the last act even I didn't, the ball goes over the fence for a six. This is me Aayush popularly known as Pappi by everyone and I like to be called as Pappi, always...

Since I understood cricket I led my neighbourhood team, I was a successful captain. I had always been passionate about captaincy. If there had been anyone who opposed my decision I played politics against that person and had him thrown out of the group.

Apart from being passionate to be a skipper, I was a charmer, a good human being, a good friend, a boy with a happy go lucky nature. All my politics ended where the sports ground ended.

I still remember that year when the seed of love for Rinki was sowed in my life. It was the occasion of *Ganesh Chaturthi*, a festival where the Hindus Worship lord Ganesha. On that auspicious day when I was sitting at the small *jhaanki* or tableaux, of our neighbourhood, I saw Harshit teasing a girl. The girl turned and started to run towards me. It was Rinki and as I saw my jaws dropped to my knees I couldn't imagine her looking so beautiful and gorgeous in her open hair with a butterfly clip holding a few streaks of her hair. She was dressed in a Royal NAVY Blue colour *Salwar Kurta* (Indian ethnic dress). I call that colour as Royal NAVY Blue as it looked awesome on Rinki; it had golden embroidery on the *Kurta and Dupatta*. Wow! She was just looking like a pretty angel running with her freshly washed hair flowing in the air like silk ribbons. She came running to me, "Pappi look Harshit is teasing me." I smiled at her cute face. Then she said, "Pappi, you are such a good boy nice and humble, why did you befriend Harshit he is not good, he will ruin you."

I couldn't forget those words, I guess that was the time my heart fell for Rinki. Although this seed of love took a long time to grow into a full plant, which was a sequence of some incidents occurred much later in my life.

One fine day entered the factor which brought turmoil into my life, the factor was Arti a girl from St. Theresa School, a prominent girl's School in BHEL Township. She came to live in our neighbourhood.

Arti was dynamic and studious girl. She belonged to that very rare species of women called, "Beauty with Brains," quite outspoken and caring as well.

One day I was sitting in veranda when I saw her looking for someone to play with; I looked at this as a potential opportunity to have a chat with her. Arti looked at me and gave a mesmerizing smile. I immediately got into the boots of SRK and was about to take the first step suddenly Harshit's voice came like '*Akashwani*' (voice from skies) and shattered the first impression created by my SRK actions. "*Abe line de rahi hai*" (Bro she is interested in you). I wanted to counter that '*Akashwani*' till heaven and shout, 'Why me?'

Harshit's words were like a pointed dagger penetrating deep inside and suddenly all my energy blew up like a high voltage transformer being short circuited. My SRK pink cheeks became blood red. Even Arti heard it; she was standing a mere 18.5 meters away from me which is a negligible distance infront of Harshit's super-sonic voice. All my high spirits evaporated, I hung my shoulders and Arti the poor creature left the very next moment. I not being able to control my temper turned to Harshit infuriating like fuming H_2SO_4, my anger knew no bounds and I spat my words at Harshit like a flamethrower throwing flames at an enemy bunker, "Why the hell on this planet you always have to make an entry whenever I am trying to achieve something with the opposite sex."

I didn't speak to Harshit the whole day and kept wondering what Arti would think about me.

Arti became a friend of Pinky my sister which I suppose was by the virtue of two same aged girls living in the same neighbourhood.

Few days later Pinky came to my house and told me that Arti was enquiring about you. That little piece of information from Pinky came to me as if someone has answered the S.O.S call to my sinking ship.

I said, "Is it so? What did she ask?"

"Ahh! Nothing much just general stuff. How is Pappi? Is he a good boy? Stuff like that."

"So what did you tell her?"

"Of course good things *bhaiya* (brother), how can I say anything bad about you?"

"Was she impressed?"

She gave me a suspicious look "I think so. But why do you look so abnormally interested. What's on your mind?"

"Just like that, whenever someone from neighbourhood asks something about you, you do get anxious to know what the reaction was, just a normal query, nothing else." Later, that night I thought will Arti be my friend. Will I be able to make a good impression in her eyes? Lost in these thoughts I slept.

Almost one week later Pinky came to my house and said in a mischievous tone "Arti wants to be your friend." These words of Pinky were like a romantic number of SRK going through my ears.

Later, that night after dinner I went to the terrace of my house stared at the sky and shouted, *"Yeeaaaahh."*

Arti and I became good friends, we both were in 9th Standard whenever she had any doubt she would come to me and ask for my notes. I without a moment of delay used to give them to her; she was even impressed by my handwriting. I always used to wonder that she is so good in studies but then why does she borrow notes from me, I guess asking for notes was her idea and a reason to talk to me. Gradually we came so close that whenever and wherever she had to go she used to take me with her that included her School stationery items shopping, snacks at local sweet shop or even at times her clothes shopping. Our relation grew to such an extent that whenever she felt that I was wrong she used to fight with me as if she was my girlfriend.

I still remember the day when we had a break-off kind of thing in between us, break-off as in we were not on talking terms and kind of because neither of us had committed to each other for being officially each other's boyfriend and girlfriend. There was a small slum near our neighbourhood and there used to be few mango and guava trees around that slum. All the boys from our neighbourhood during holidays, used to go there plucking mangoes and guavas. Arti came to knew about this and asked me not to go there, I denied her.

"You don't care what I feel and never will care about what I say to you." These words pissed me off.

"What do you think of yourself? You have no right to tell me what should I do and what I shouldn't? You are just a friend, not girlfriend." Hearing these words from me her tank of tears opened its flood gates and everything got washed out by her tears and then she ran off to her home.

Later that evening when I returned home from mango and guava adventures, I saw my mom and Arti waiting for me at the front gate of my home. My stomach immediately felt the crunches as I sensed something has exploded in my home. Arti had complained to my mom about my adventures of mango. My mom was furious and I was bombarded with shouts, shoots and bombs of scolding. Along with them came two special Air-to-Air missiles of slaps, smack!

I felt humiliated and my anger on Arti knew no limits. May be she enjoyed when my mom scolded me but when I got the slap, her face turned sorry for me. She started feeling guilty about her deed. She tried to talk to me and say sorry to me after this incident. But I decided not to talk to her and ignored her.

One day she wrote a letter to me or rather a love letter to me. That was the first love letter of my life, which I received. Arti tried to send that letter to me through my younger brother, but as usual the good luck fuel ran out and the letter ended up in my father's hand. The letter was written somewhat like this:

"My Dear Pappi,

I am sorry for what I did. I didn't know that this would hurt you so much that you would stop talking to me. My intentions were good for you; I have never thought badly for you and I have always prayed for you and that's why I told Aunty about your going near that slum area. Please don't be mad at me. I just feel like crying, everyone calls me to play with them but I don't feel like playing with them because you will leave if I come to play. I'm sorry kaan pakad ke, and I just want to tell you that I LOVE U... sorry sorry sorry...

Yours

Arti"

My Dad read the letter, but instead of hitting or scowling at me he was calm in explaining it to me and said, "Son this is not the right age for this love business. If you enter all this at this age God knows what will happen in future." He did not scold me or hit me. I guess most Indian fathers don't behave like this with their sons. Dad called Arti and calmly spoke to her, "*Beta,* this is not the right time for all this." He once again made us friends. Thanks Dad for that.

Arti and I became friends once again, but I always displayed that I am not *senti* (sentimental) about her. Whenever she asked me to accompany her to some place I denied in the most possible flat tone I could. This of course hurt her. Once she was asked by her mom to go flour mill and get the paste for making Idli, as usual she called me to accompany her to the flour mill but I refused to go with her. She asked Harshit to accompany her and that idiot Harshit did so. This made me jealous, but I couldn't go directly to Harshit and say that. I didn't like that, even after having a clue about what was going on between me and Arti he went with her.

After a few days Harshit came to me and asked, “What is the matter, why are you not talking to me?” I told him that I was hurt about that day when he went with Arti to the flour mill. He said, *“Dost (friend)* you should have told me then and there; I would not have gone with her.”

“Its okay, but from now on please don’t go with her, it’s only me who will go with her whenever or wherever it is needed.” He nodded.

This entire episode created distances between Arti and me. Although with time I forgave Arti, but somewhere at the back of my mind I never forgot this whole thing, my behaviour towards Arti continued to be rude. To Arti all of this was like being in a concentration camp where she was being mentally tortured for a severe treacherous crime. One day Arti called Pinky and asked her to somehow send me to her house. Of course she wanted to apologize. Same day in evening I entered Arti's house. I saw no one, that very instance Arti entered the living room. She was looking stunning in her white t-shirt printed with Barbie dolls and deep blue coloured denim. She said, “Hi”

“Hi”

“How are you?”

"Fine, thanks"

"Isn't anybody home?" I enquired

"No. Please sit, I'll get some *sharbat* (Indian beverage)." I sat down on the sofa and started surfing through the channels. Arti came back with two glasses of *sharbat* in a tray. She sat down next to me. My mind was getting unstable all this while. My thoughts said "Why the fuck is she looking so beautiful? Why did she call me here when her parents are not around?" All these thoughts were arousing me. After several seconds of killing silence Arti said, "Sorry *Jaan* (my life)!" My brain couldn't analyse the word *'Jaan'*. I was stunned. I looked blankly at Arti. Arti held my hand and said, "I'm really sorry about everything, please forgive me."

"I have already dismissed that issue from my heart please don't make me feel guilty by mentioning that." As I said these my eyes met Arti's. Arti held my hand so tight that I could feel the grip on my heart. The distance between us was getting eliminated. With that the distance between our lips was getting erased. When my upper lip touched Arti's lower lip all the differences in our relationship were wiped off. The kiss was so passionate that I wished time would stop right here forever. I was filled with that first touch of kiss in life. All those scenes I saw in some blue film shown by Harshit started rushing into my mind. Well it was dirty thoughts, but when a girl like Arti is in your arms; who wants clean thoughts. Our hands were exploring each other through the waists, beneath the cover of clothes. Arti's softness really had turned me on, the dusky golden colour of Arti's skin was the most appealing thing on this planet to me; I slid my plam into her top, rushing to unhook her.

She said, "Easy rocket, there's no hurry to land on the moon," I grinned.

It took me five thousand seconds to unhook her; Arti's eyes were a mix of inhibition and mischief. All of this to me was like the first night after wedding, full of love intensity and flavour of mischief. Looking at her body excited me, the touch of it ignited the fire in her. I kissed her to the fullest. Her tender lips, her curvaceous body, every kiss I planted on her made her moan to the highest level of ecstacy. As I freed her body from the grip of her clothes and looked at her, she looked like the Goddess of love. Her soft skin and perfectly curved body acted like a magnet for my mind and body, I explored every corner of her body with my hands. I couldn't satisfy my desire for her by just kissing every inch of her body. I wanted more of her; all of her for myself. Her ignited body had turned her on so much that by now she was exploring every inch of my body with her hands. I loved the touch of her on my body and soul. As she undressed me, I kept exploring the corners of her body with my kisses and she did the same for me. We were drawn towards each and wanted to completely submerse ourselves in each other. The air gap between us vanished as we stuck to each other like lovers of eternal destiny.

One day when I came back after winning a cricket match, I went directly to Arti to give her the good news, I saw that she was not as chirpy and enthusiastic as she was normally. My sixth sense told me there was something bad coming up.

She told me that her Dad has rented a new house and they are moving there. Her words came like a jolt of lightening to me I could hardly contain the water droplets in my eyes; I rushed back home.

Later that night after dinner although I could hardly eat, I went to my terrace looked up and asked, “Why Me?” A tear escaped from my eyes.

A week later Arti moved out of the neighbourhood and I could just keep Anupam and my favourite song by smokie played in the background which we often sing till date, “I don’t know why she's leaving or where she's gonna go, I guess she’s got her reasons but I just don’t want to know, coz for twenty four years I have been living next door to ...”

These were some of the glimpses of me as a lover who was always unsuccessful but was liked by all the girls, I would say I was *bhondhu* (dumbo) who at the right time was not able to understand girls feelings otherwise the story would have been a bit different, but at least that gave me the reason involved to narrate the second chapter of this book because of all such unsuccessful attempts of love by me at that age.

3

PAPPT AKA AAYUSH KUMAR - PART 2

BHOOT: - THE GHOST:

After Arti left my behaviour changed towards all girls, whenever a girl spoke nicely to me, I got infatuated. I dreamt about her all the time. To say the truth I liked being in such dreams as they don't hurt anyone and when it came to my knowledge that she has started to see someone my heart was smashed or rather the infatuation was. I could never discuss or say all these things to anyone except Anupam he used to laugh and say, *"Tera naam Aayush nahi Ashiq hona chahiye tha, tera koi bharosa nahi aaj Arti kal koi dooja* (Your name should be lover and not Aayush, you are so capricious today Arti tomorrow someone else). But don't worry I'm sure you will soon find the meaning of true love in your life."

One evening while playing cricket, the guys of my neighbourhood started gossiping about Rinki. I overheard strange things happening at Rinki's home.

Later that night I asked my mom and whatever she told me was shocking. Mom told me someone did a *puja* at the *chauraha* (crossroads) and threw away some lemons and green chillies on the road which were allegedly enchanted with ghostly spells and while coming back from School by mistake Rinki stepped on them and since then is behaving strangely. People rompingly said that some *ramlaal chamaar's* (ramlal the shoemaker) ghost has entered her body. I felt very bad, I liked her and I had very good friendship with her. I wanted to help Rinki in any way I could.

Next day I started off for Rinki's house to meet her. Suddenly I heard a loud scream and it was sure that was not human. It came from Rinki's house. I sprinted.

As I entered her house the sound became louder. Her father and brother were scared like hell; all their faces were white like a sheet. I went towards her room, I could feel that I was getting nervous and was losing my balance; suddenly I felt lot of power in myself and moved straight into her room.

The scene inside her room was unexplainable. She was about two feet above her bed. “Oh! My god!” I was surely not living in a world of humans. Her voice was not the soft Rinki’s voice it was more like a man's voice.

Suddenly her father gave her 2 tight slaps. If it would have been someone else and under normal circumstances I would have broken the hand of the person to touch her, but this was no normal situation, I just wanted to shout *no uncle please don’t hit her, she is very special to me.* But I controlled myself as her Dad hit his lovely princess for her well being. I said, “Uncle we should do something to stop her, hitting her will hurt Rinki and not the ghost which is inside her.” After sometime she went silent and slept.

Her father called a *tantrik* (sorcerer) next day and after much *puja* and *Jhad–Funk* he gave her a *tabeez* (pendent). After few days she became normal, but that incident had wrecked her.

One day I went to meet her. When I saw her she was very depressed. She said, “Pappi I don’t go any where because people stare at me, as if I have committed some crime and it makes me feel guilty. Is it my fault that all this happened to me?” She burst into tears and kept her head on my shoulder. I could feel my shirt getting wet with her tears; I gently brushed her hair and let her cry. After her tears stopped rolling out of those beautiful eyes, I held her hand and she followed me. She was so confused, just like a small baby with tears rolling on her cheeks looking so confused and cute. I said, "Trust me and come with me." She followed me like a baby. As we went out people started their talks, making strange faces, but we kept walking. After taking a short walk I dropped her at her home. After that day I took her out everyday that week but we never spoke to each other just walked along together. One day when we were walking Rinki firmed her grip, I looked at her and she said, "You take me out for a walk everyday and you just keep walking so silently along with me. I know people see us and make fun of you to be with me but you still walk with me. I feel good walking with you I feel as if nothing will harm me anymore. But why don't you say something, why do you just keep walking silently?"

"Rinki I just want you to understand and remember one thing I will always be there for you. I don't speak because I want you to feel that when I am walking with you and nothing will harm you. Whenever you are in trouble I want you to look around and you will always find a friend who will stand by you, no matter what. I won't shout like others to make my presence felt around you, it's my support which should make you feel my presence around and I don't care what people say I know the girl who is standing with me is the most beautiful, cute and innocent girl I have ever seen in my life. I just walk with you being your support. That is why I walk in silence along with you."

She went speechless and closed her eyes. That moment a tear of happiness escaped her beautiful pink eye lids. That evening I walked all the time with Rinki holding my hand in her soft little palms the warmth of which made love blossom in my heart. Those words from me gave her a lot of confidence.

I passed my 10th board exams with distinction and it was again summer vacations. We were already in our late teens. Rinki's frequency for playing decreased following her family's instructions and she spent time at home. But I could not stop thinking about her and my heart had already been filled by her lovely thoughts.

SUMMERS:

Both Anupam and I were to take admission in 11th standard and also choose our subject stream. The options which we had were science, commerce and arts. My family always wanted to see me pursuing my career as an engineer so they insisted for Physics, Chemistry and Mathematics. I decided to go with PCM stream as I had scored 99 out of 100 marks in 10th standard Mathematics. All other friends of my locality Pankaj, Chintu, Rakhi, Rinki took commerce.

My Dad went to Raman School for collecting the admission forms and there he met the Principal the great Mishra Sir. Mishra Sir looked at my 10th marksheet which had distinction marks in all the subjects and asked my father that he wants to talk to me. Next day I went to meet him. He asked me "Are you joining this School for fun?" I was shocked to hear all this but I controlled myself and with good acting skills told him, "No sir absolutely not. Everyone knows that the highest number of MPPET entrance and IIT JEE entrance selections are from this School. I am joining here because I want good guidance to crack the entrance exams."

"Very well fine then I will consider you to get admitted here in this School but if ever I catch you with those bad boys or doing any such mischief then I will expel you from the School."

"Yes Sir."

It was decided that Anupam and I would be joining Raman with PCM as subject stream. But then again my capricius mind got diverted as Rinki came to my mind. I came to know that Rinki had taken commerce so I thought even I would take commerce so that way I can go to the same coaching where Rinki would go and be close to her.

I told My Dad that I wanted to take commerce. Dad had no objection to it. We went to Mishra Sir and asked him for change of subject.

Mishra Sir said, “You got 99 in Maths and still you want to take commerce, beta give it a thought.”

“Sir I have decided I want to take admission in commerce this is my final decision.”

The Principal then said to my father, “Okay I will change the stream in admission form but tell me something sir, is your boy mad?”

Now since I was in the same School as Anupam was and in the same stream as Rinki was, I felt good about it. After this my relatives said PCM is good and there are lots of opportunities in PCM, like be an engineer or I could do B.Sc in physics or Chemistry or Mathematics or I could even move to do B.Com. I agreed on the condition that after 12th grade I shall not be forced by anyone to which stream or college I join.

The next day I went to Mishra Sir and requested him to change my stream in the admission form once again. The Principal got furious. "What is this? Is it a joke whenever you wish you come to change your stream? Now it is not possible and we are already in the final stages of the admission procedure. Nothing can be done now." After sometime he cooled down and said "Beta, this is the last time I am changing it now if you change your mind I will cancel your admission form. Go work hard and make your career."

After all this drama of admission Anupam and I were confident of getting selected and decided to celebrate with beer at a *dhaba* (Eatery on the highway). Again Alcohol was something which we recently started and had still not become regular consumers of that wonder liquid which Anupam says 'Man's greatest and most beautiful creation'.

A week later on Wednesday I had to go to Anupam's place as our admission results were to come out. I had my bath, prayed to God. This was something which is not common between Anupam and me, Anupam is an Atheist or an Agnostic guy. After praying I looked at the watch, 'Oh! I was getting late'. I was to get ready to go to School but before that there was one thing which I always did, that was on my old tape-recorder I played SRK's romantic song "*Tujhe dekha toh yeh jaana sanam*" and came out of my room at the verandah giving a SRK glare at Rinki's house as this was the time on Monday morning during summers when she used to go to the temple.

That day My Dad was at home and when he saw me standing in the veranda with the SRK actions he asked me, *"Yaha kyu khada hai* (Why are you standing here)? *Waiting for someone?"*

"No one Dad."

My father used to tease me every time I used to get ready to go out, as if I am going to chase girls.

Finally she came. I played the song in highest volume my oldie had. As she passed by my home she gave one of those assassin smiles. The moment was like as if I won the *Filmfare* award and kissed the award.

Quickly I got out of my home and started to follow her, I followed her till the local bus stop, then she went the other way for temple and I pedalled my way towards Anupam's house.

I reached Anupam's house, I saw he was ready and waiting for me. This was one of his qualities which not everyone in India has; "Punctuality." He is 99% on time every time and he expects the same, but I used to disappoint him as I am late 99% of time. As I reached his place he was furious at me and was fuming at me, I had to say sorry a zillion times after which he said, "Okay fine now let's move now."

After pedalling for 15-20 minutes we reached Raman. There were a lot of students near the notice board to check out the admission results, most of them were commerce stream aspirants.

We went to the notice board which read, 'PCM Admission List'. As we scrolled down the list we found Anupam's name on the list at with section C allotted to him, then we scrolled down the list, to much disappointment I couldn't find my name on the first page. I thought may be Mishra Sir got too fed up with my requests for changes in stream and he denied me the admission in his School. I thought "damn him!"

As we scrolled through we reached the last page of the list and my heart sank. I thought 'I am ruined because of my confusion.' I was lost in these thoughts just then Anupam shouted, "Bingo! Here you are mate." I couldn't believe my name was there against a scholar number and roll number 2 and more importantly section C was allotted to me.

4

SCHOOL OF DREAMS

RAMAN – PART 1

Welcome back. Oh! I mean this is Anupam talking to you again. The rest of the story you'll have to bear in my narration.

JULY 1997:

First day at Raman Higher Secondary School. Pappi and I decided to meet at the roundabout in front of our School at 9.30 A.M. the School started at 10.00 A.M.

I reached the roundabout at sharp 9.30 A.M. and Pappi as usual arrived 15 minutes late. He came with Rana.

As Pappi reached I felt like shouting at him for being late, but as he came he said, "Sorry, please *yaar,* you know that no matter how hard I try, I can never be on time, and everyone does not follow time like you do, you are too punctual to be in India."

"Okay next time make sure you are not late more than 5 minutes."

"Done"

"Okay now let's go it's almost time for the morning assembly to begin."

Rana my cousin said, "Wait we still got 18 minutes, lets have a quick smoke before we go." I objected to that. Rana insisted, "C'mon guys who cares what time of day is it and who knows whether on the first day we would be able to break the walls and come out for a smoke."

I gave in but asked him to make it quick. Quickly Rana got our brand, the great brand of all times the one and only *WILLS NAVY CUT*. All three of us quickly dragged the cigarette.

Pappi said, "Hey dude aren't you guys excited?"

"Why?"

"C'mon yaar Raman is a co-ed School and there must be a lot of girls around." Raman was a co-ed School and Raman was the only School left among all schools of BHEL Education Society to not have switched to (Central Board of Secondary

Education) (CBSE) syllabus, so there was every chance that girls from even Radhakrishnan School would be moving to Raman for the state board education syllabus. As SRK Pappi was always ready to get senti and instantaneously fall in love with every girl he saw and who behaved nice with her.

After the quick drag which took 10 minutes of the remaining 18 minutes, we grabbed a *Chutki* (a mouth freshener available in India) each and rushed off. Bingo! We had messed it up again and we were late on the very first day of our new School. As we reached the corridor which led to the ground we saw all classes lined up for the assembly and all teachers also present at the ground. Damn it, because a stupid idea of smoking on an early morning we missed the assembly the very first day.

I said, “Hey guys did you notice that Mishra Sir is not on the stage.”

Pappi asked with a confusion, “Yes, so what?”

“It’s okay that he is not on stage, but don’t you guys think that on the first day of the new academic year of the School the Principal is supposed to be on the stage and address the public gathering.”

Rana said, “May be he is on a round of the School and will come and address the assembly after the regular assembly is over." Pappi looked at him and his facial expression changed from confusion to fear, "Oh shit no ways man, I got to look somewhere to hide, I can't get caught by him on the very first day, he will kick my butt out of the School the very first day."

I said, "Chill lets see what's happening." Just then I heard a noise behind us. I looked back four students were coming towards us, one of them was Prashant Channe, he had studied with us for one year at St' Xavier's. Prashant came and said, "Hi, you guys late too."

I said, "No we wanted to have the spectacular view of the assembly from the corridor that's why we are hiding here."

"Okay never mind, but I hear that the Principal is late today so may be he won't come today." Hearing this all of us were relieved.

Pappi asked, "But how are we going to get to our class, we even don't know which Classroom is our section."

Suddenly one of the guys shouted "*Mishra Sir aa gaye* (Mishra Sir has come)." These words came like thunderbolt to our ears we turned and we saw Mishra Sir out of his *Maruti 800.*

Without thinking for a moment all seven of us rushed into the boys' washroom and everyone maintained pin drop silence. Mishra Sir went straight to the assembly. There was a small window in the boys' washroom from where we could keep an eye on the proceedings.

Rana said, "The Principal is busy in the assembly and will be delivering his lecture soon, why don't we go out of this toilet and hide somewhere else."

Prashant replied, "Don't even think of it, if you go outside now you will be caught red handed, there's one demon standing outside, his name is Paramlal. He is the security of this School and the most dreaded character. Seniors say that he was once a constable with M.P Police and now after retiring he is in our School." So we had to wait here inside a washroom till we got the suitable opportunity to get out. After the assembly was dismissed we moved out and along with other students went to our class.

The class was still without a teacher and the students had already made the class a fish market with their chit chat as we entered everyone looked at us and we looked around for girls but once again fate was not on our side. Pappi's heart broke even before meeting a girl, and contrary to our hopes the class had a completely different image that of the deserts of Rajasthan where there's only hot sand, no greenery and no water, only mirages of water and greenery. There were only two girls in our class.

One was a Chinese looking girl named Naina and the other one was called Sangita.

In a few moments a professor entered our class, he did not look like a professor he looked more like a PhD student. He was quite tall my best guess would be 6'2'' tall and somewhere close to 80 or 85 kilograms. He came into the class with a copy of physics book by R.B. Tripathi and addressed the class, "I'm Binu Jacob, your class teacher and your physics teacher. I will be taking all your physics classes except Optics as that will be covered by another professor, whom you will meet shortly. Is that okay?"

We said, "Yes Sir."

After a brief round of introductions we started with the dimensional analysis, which most of the students found tough and boring. But to me physics was heaven and I loved the subject. The remaining day went pretty eventless with regular classes going on and at 4.30 P.M the final School bell rang and we went home. After having a light lunch and some rest I started off for my coaching at 5.30 P.M.

On Thursday during lunch I said, "Pappi *yaar,* its getting more boring here than St' Xavier's, we heard that Raman is known for the adventures it gives to its students, but where is all the adventure."

Pappi said "I know dude, even I am wondering where all the adventure is." After lunch when we went to our class I noticed that a couple of guys who came from Vikram were missing.

I said, "Pappi where are those two guys who were sitting next to us."

"Yes dude they are missing." After some enquiry we came to know that the guys have escaped from School at lunch hour. So the adventures of 11th 'C' had begun.

We decided to participate but we needed expert advice, do our analysis and then undertake our first adventure as none of us wanted to get caught up in the act and get kicked out of the School just because we did not have adequate information on what to do and how to do.

The next lecture was of Hindi and the professor was an old lady named Mrs. Gogia who preferred sitting on the chair and taking us through the chapters and was least bothered about what was going on at the last bench.

I asked Prashant, "Have you ever escaped from the School?"

"Yes, but not much and even I do not have much knowledge about it."

"Then who does?"

"Try asking the guys from Vikram School they are specially trained for these things." I looked around for someone from Vikram School and saw my old St. Xavier's classmate Vipin Sarode sitting two rows in front of me. I called him in a loud whisper; he looked back. I gesticulated with my palm to come to my desk. He under cover of the poor eyesight of the Hindi teacher slipped from his desk and came to my desk and I asked, "We need information."

Vipin looked puzzled, "What information?"

"Information on bunking classes" Vipin laughed at it and for next 45 minutes explained everything in detail from being physically fit for jumping walls of 10-12 feet high to sprinting to parking bicycles outside of School.

Next Monday, during the assembly, as I approached the queues of students in order of their class and I was surprised on what I saw or rather whom I saw, it was Rekha standing in front of the queue of 11th 'B'. I just paused there for a moment looking at her, it was kind of awkward and embarrassing for me. I noticed that when she looked at me or perhaps my open mouth standing right in front of the stage and she passed a short giggle, I squirmed a bit and then quickly I was off to the end of the queue of my section. After the assembly by the time I reached my classroom being at the end of the queue Rekha was already at her seat and to my astonishment she took the window seat on the side of the passage. I wondered that would this be her regular seat, as I passed the window of her class I just kept looking at her.

I entered my class and took my seat with Pappi and Pappi saw the streak of happiness on my face and asked, “What?”

I looked at him, “What is what?”

“What is the reason for that streak of smile on your damned face?”

“Not what, it’s who.” Hearing this even Rana turned his neck around to look at me.

Pappi asked, “No way! You must be kidding.”

I smiled.

He asked, “Which section is she in?”

“Well the shocking stuff is she is our next door neighbour.”

Pappi screamed out, “What?”

“*isssshhhhhhhhh*!”

“What? Now really you got to be kidding. She is our next door neighbour and we didn’t even notice it.”

“Maybe she joined classes late.”

"You are lucky that Rekha is in the next class I wish Rinki would have been in same School and in my next door section I would have been head over heels on it."

Rana interfered, "Can you two talk about it later, now what about the escaping mission."

I said, "Well the best option is the near fence wall of labs. The section where the corridor takes a left towards labs, there this main building ends and the smaller third part of the building starts, we can go up to there and then make a small sprint to the wall, the wall is also not too high it must be around 7 feet."

Pappi said, "Lets take one more day for reconnaissance and then we do it on Wednesday."

D-DAY:

The next day was our D-Day to execute the mission. That morning we parked our bikes outside the School premises and walked inside our School.

During lunch we moved out of our class with our School bags on our shoulders and kept roaming around the sports ground along with other students. Rekha saw us with bags; she gave a suspicious glance at us and then went. Just as the bell rang we started our slow walk towards the drinking water bay. After reaching the drinking water bay we saw a few students still there. We were in no hurry so we let everyone quench their thirst and then we went to the taps. After wasting five minutes at the taps, we were done with the drinking water bay phase of our mission. I turned around and said, "Oh Shit." As I saw Mishra Sir coming out of his room, I said, "Quick inside the toilet." All three of us rushed into the boys' toilet. As Mishra Sir went on his round for the School we waited. Damn! How can we expect to do anything adventurous without running into trouble and this was our first escapade mission and here we were locked and hiding once again in the boys washroom. I peeped out and saw Mishra Sir going upstairs for his round. I said, "Okay boys, let's go."

We started our walk slowly then gradually increased our speed to a limit where any onlooker would not doubt our mission as we had to pass by several classes; even ours. As we crossed our class passage which was almost the centre of the corridor I again looked towards the window of Rekha, she noticed us moving towards the mission zone, I wished that she would come and *tilak* (a vermillion decoration on the forehead for Hindus) me like a warrior going for a battle for undertaking such a dangerous mission.

As we reached the section where the main building ended and the corridor took a 90 degree left turn, we turned right towards the wall. On my green signal all three of us sprinted towards the wall with our bags on our shoulders, I guess that sprint must have been so fast that if we continued that way we would have made one kilometre in just 3 minutes or may be less. Pappi took the right side of a pillar and Rana took the left, I waited behind Rana I pushed his butt from behind and said, "C'mon *chutiye,* lift your ass up that damn wall." As Rana climbed up the wall and after him I. By this time Pappi had already made his jump and was rolling on the ground. After that Rana did his jump and then rolled on the ground and as I climbed up the fence exactly putting my left leg on the middle horizontal bar and climbed the pillar, as I reached the top of the pillar I thought, 'Boy this is way too high, even I'm going to roll on the ground.' I made my jump, landed on the ground with a big thud and immediately bent my knees to allow for the impact to be absorbed, my legs felt a tremor run through them, surprisingly I managed to avoid roll on the ground but couldn't get up so soon as I was already on my knees on the ground. After a few seconds I got up and sprinted off to the place where we parked our bicycles, picking our bicycles we headed for the main market of the area where the School was located. After we were out of danger, we stopped at a local *Pan–Tapri* (Roadside shop for cigarettes) to celebrate our first escape mission from School to be successful and as we got off from our bikes, we hugged each other and this time we bought 3 *WILLS NAVY CUT* one for each and as we lighted them took our first puff we brought all the three cigarettes together to say CHEERS!

CUPID STRIKES - LOVE ENTERS:

It was the end of July in 1997 when one day Pappi did not come to School; Rana and I were in no mood to attend classes or practicals or whatever was there in School. We planned a movie.

At around 12:45 P.M. we sneaked out of the School, took our bikes and set off in the direction of Jyoti talkies. On our way to Jyoti talkies we stopped at a signal; just then a Maruti Gypsy came and screeched by our side at the signal. That was a government of India vehicle. I looked into the Gypsy; I went in a fairy tale dream. I saw the most beautiful girl of my life ever. I had never seen such a beautiful face ever. She was an angel. The moment I saw her I fell in love with her. Indeed that was love at first sight, a love which at that moment I didn't know will change my life forever. She was from Convent School. That was my first glance of the girl who would change my life forever.

That night I couldn't sleep, there was just one thing on my mind, that girl; there was only one face in my eyes, hers. I just kept wondering who she was. But the more important question in my mind was how can anyone be so beautiful to make one fall in love in seconds?

The next day there was a sparkle in my eyes and why not I was in love. Pappi noticed it and asked, “What?”

“I’m in love.”

“I knew some day you will fall in love with her. So when are you telling her?”

“I don’t know. I don’t even know who she is or where does she live? How can I propose her without knowing all that?”

“What do you mean by you don’t know? We know where she lives. She is in the classroom next door and comes to our coaching classes daily. Propose to her today after the classes.”

I stared at him in anguish and asked, “Whom are you talking about?”

“Of course Rekha”

“No dude you are getting it all wrong. She is not Rekha.”

“What the fuck! Who the fuck is it then!” I narrated the whole incident which happened the day before and how last night I couldn’t sleep thinking about that girl.

Pappi said, “Wow cool love story bud. Are you nuts? How can you fall in love in seconds and on top of that with a girl from Convent, don’t you know how those girls are and this girl you are talking about seems to be the daughter of some bureaucrat. Dude you will get all of our asses kicked hard. I think you should consider Rekha, proposing her is much safer as far as *panga* (picking up fights) is concerned."

"Dude its love, not a bike or a business deal to think about safety."

"Fine, by the way how does this lovely girl look like?"

"Stunning, enchanting, she is Venus."

Before the last lecture before lunch, I said to Pappi, "Dude I'm out." Pappi gave me a puzzled look.

I said, "It's time for her School to be over and she would be and she would be leaving for her home, so I can go there again and see her."

"Fine let's go then." We again sneaked out of School and pedalled our way towards Convent School as I reached the same signal I said to Pappi, "Dude we are going to wait here for her."

That day even after waiting for 45 minutes I couldn't see her, Pappi kept cursing me for falling in love with a girl I saw for a few seconds.

5

MISSON IMPOSSIBLE

Overconfidence and Ambushed in Action

With the festival of *Durga Puja* (One the of three biggest Hindu festivals and the biggest for Bengalis) just around the corner festive moods were going on high spirits and especially for me it meant more fun and enjoyment as I belonged to a Bengali family and this festival is the most important festival for all Bengalis.

It was Monday the 6th of October 1997; we as usual reached School after lunch escaped from School and went to one of our adda the woods near the School when Rana said, "Hey lets go for a *Durga Puja* tableaux visit around the city tomorrow."

I said, "Okay, but why tomorrow, we can do that in the coming 4 days when the festival is in its full glamour."

"Yes we can, but you know it's the peak rush hour during those four days and we may not be able to see all the tableaux's in those four days, so we can go and visit some of them in tomorrow when they are comparatively less crowded or not at all crowded and some of them are even giving final touches to their decorations." Rana had a point there in saying that during those four days of *Shashti, Saptami, Ashtami and Navami* (6th, 7th, 8th and 9th days of the festival) all the tableaux's were over crowded and one had to be in a queue to enter them.

Pappi said, "Fine we can do that, but then why not go for it today, why tomorrow?"

Rana said, "Reason is we can't risk moving around the whole city in our School uniforms where in anyone and everyone can see us and God forbid if any of our uncles locate us who might contributing his part of labour for decorating the tableaux then we are killed and that too if we are located roaming around the city in our School uniforms then dude we are killed on the spot." This made sense and indeed we were scared of getting spotted by some uncle of ours.

Pappi said, "Okay, we go tomorrow, but then how do we get rid of this uniform."

Rana said, “Simple carry a civil shirt or t-shirt after escaping from School we change our shirts and then move on.”

The next day 7th of October 1997 was the fateful day, normally days having number 7 are lucky for me as I was born on 7th. But that day was the first of the two instances when I would remember a day with date 7th. After the assembly we went to our classes and the first lecture was of our class teacher Binu Jacob. During the lecture we were finalizing our plans; two of our classmates one Prashant Upadhyay and Solanki heard us.

Upadhyay asked, “Can we join in too?”

I asked, “What do you mean by we?”

“Solanki and I.”

“Buddy I don’t worry about you, but will Solanki be able to do it?” Solanki’s height was too short to jump a 10 or 12 feet wall.

Solanki said, “Don’t worry I have done it a few times in Vikram, so I can do it here as well.” I looked at Pappi and Rana, they nodded in agreement.

I said, “Okay you guys can join us. The plan is to escape from the long range wall first and then we shall decide which place to go first to start our tableaux tour.”

After the class got over and Binu Jacob left for the staff room we started our walk a good ten paces behind him so that he doesn't watch us moving out of the class. We reached the stage which was good 25–30 yards away from the ground and was directly visible from the staff room. Without any signal or say Solanki started his sprint towards the ground, seeing this Rana also started his sprint and Upadhyay also did the same. Pappi and I looked at each other and said, "What the fuck, this was not the plan!" Then we realized that we were in direct visual range of the staff room and this is no point to have WHAT WENT WRONG analysis and we too have to run off. We both said in unison "OH SHIT" and started our sprint. By the time we reached the wall Rana and Upadhyay had crossed over to the other side and Solanki was finding a hard time to jump over the wall as we reached I pushed his butt and he was over the wall. Then both Pappi and I climbed the wall and crossed over. After crossing over we were safe and felt as if we had been successful in dodging trouble once again. I was really furious at Solanki for this stupidity of his.

I yelled at Solanki, *"Fucker*! Why the hell did you run from the stage, do you realize that me and Pappi were in trouble because of this act of yours you damn fool!" By this time Rana and Pappi had already begun their walk towards the cycle parking.

Upadhyay came to me, "*Chhod naa yaar* (leave is buddy), whatever had to happen has happened now tell what to do next?"

"Nothing just pick the bikes; change your shirts and get moving." As we were about to follow Rana and Pappi towards the parking a LML scooter came from behind us. I could not believe my eyes it was BINU JACOB our class teacher on that scooter with another lecturer whom we called Gattu Mishra seated behind. We just stood there, no we froze there. Rana and Pappi had the chance to run away as they were few paces ahead of us but they did not, they came back. I knew that was because we had the most wonderful relation in the world between us called friendship. As Binu Jacob stopped the scooter Gattu Mishra approached us and tore off a branch of a bush to use it as stick against us for self defence as if he was scared that we would beat the hell out of him. He was jumping with that stick in his hands like a monkey, who jumps when his master tells him to. But Binu Jacob was quite. He came to us and took our bags from us and said, "Come and collect it from the Principal's office." After this they went away. I was cursing Solanki for his immature act of running from in front of the staff room. Binu Jacob and Gattu Mishra must have definitely spotted five commandos in Raman

Uniform coming out of class and make their heroic run towards freedom.

We had two options either to forget our belongings and run away and then don't turn up for School for the next two months or to go and meet the Principal who from Mishra Sir must have become *Hatyara* (killer) Mishra; waiting for us to enter his den and then kill his prey.

I said, "What do we do now?"

Pappi said, "Man I am screwed up. They will call my Dad and my Dad will kill me. I'm done with schooling dudes."

Rana said, "Lets run away and we don't turn up for School for next few weeks and the issue will go down."

I said, "Great idea! Excellent! But do you remember that he has got our bags with him and those bags have our School diaries in them which has got our complete bio–data they will directly call our Dad's and then we all are doomed." Our mission had been ambushed and now we had no option but to go to the killer's den.

I said, "We don't have any option let's go back to School."

Solanki said, "Let's go back by jumping the wall again why to walk so much round the road to reach the main gate."

We all stared at him.

"Okay fine let's walk."

Thus we started our lone walk as defeated commandos of an army who had been taken prisoners of war in a mission and were now on their way to the concentration camp where they would be beaten and given 3rd degree treatment to bring out important enemy information.

As we reached the main gate the *chaukidar* (gatekeeper) stopped us and asked, "What is it?"

I said, "We have to meet Mishra Sir." He didn't say anything and let us go in, probably he must have known by now that we were the commandos who were taken prisoners; he must have seen this 'n' number of times in his life as the chaukidar of Raman. As we went in Binu Jacob and Gattu Mishra were already inside the Principal's den. On seeing us Mishra Sir gave us a killing look; as a lion looks at a lamb that has come to his den knowing there is no other option but to get killed. As we five entered Gattu Mishra closed the door behind us, which sent a shiver down my spine. The Principal stood up and came to us and said, "*Kya yehi hain who*? (Are they the ones?)"

Bloody Gattu Mishra said, "Yes Sir."

All of us were standing there with our heads down. Before I could understand anything BANG! Came the first blow to my cheeks, then came another and then it was like a rain of slaps on my cheeks, for almost two minutes I was standing there in that rain of slaps and there was no umbrella here to save me from that, my cheeks had already gone numb from those hits. In those two minutes I must have scored 25–30 of those hard slaps from the Principal. It was Rana's turn now and here too without any warning he rained slaps on him BANG! BANG! BANG! But he did not get much of the thrashing hardly 10–15 of hard hits; well 10–15 hits are less when you compare it with my 25-30 hits. Then it was Pappi who got around ten hits; Upadhayay got around 5–8 of them and the last Solanki the major culprit he got only bloody 2–3 hits on his face. Just when the Principal was done with his hard hitting that bloody Gattu Mishra again spoke from the back, "*Sir yeh dono toh roz bhagte hai*" (Sir, these two run away from School daily) and pointed towards Me and Rana. The Principal again came to me and asked, "Why you run away from School." by the time he finished this statement 5-6 more hard hits had already landed upon me making the count to 30-35 hits. Then he said, "Bring me your diaries I will call your Dad right away." As Binu Jacob opened my bag he found my printed green coloured shirt in my bag which I had brought to change my School uniform. Gattu Mishra snatched my shirt and shouted, "Sir there is a shirt in his bag." Oh my goodness; for fuck's sake why did that fucker Gattu had to yell out in such a way that would bring more of Mishra Sir's fury on me. BANG! Again a hard hit on my face and he asked, "Tell me where you go after running away from School? Tell me? Are you into drugs? Tell me, I demand an explanation right now."

"No sir I go straight home after running away from School." BANG! Came another blow on my face.

"You damn liar, tell me the truth, if you go straight home then why is this shirt in your School bag."

"No sir I am not into drugs. I go home; straight to home from School, this shirt is in my bag because Sir I have my tuitions early in the morning and I leave my home in civil dress. After my tuitions I change into School uniform and then come here Sir. I swear on the idol of *maa saraswati* (mother goddess of learning) kept here sir and after going home I study and prepare for my MPPET exams sir." BANG! Came another bloody blow this time it wrecked my jaw line completely.

"What do you think? The teachers in Raman are incompetent that you need to go for external tuitions. The teachers here can't give you enough guidance and preparation for competitive exams." BANG! BANG! BANG! BANG! came four more blows by this I was completely devastated and my jaw structure went completely numb the hits count must have been somewhere close to half century. He then asked Pappi, "You tell me why you ran from School?"

"Sir I was having fever sir, so wanted to go home." BANG! BANG!

"You had fever and still you managed to sprint off to that wall from the classroom and then you even managed to jump off that damn 10 feet high wall. *Itne bukhaar mein bhi kood gaye?* (How did you jump with fever?)" BANG!

Mishra Sir then said those golden words which we remember even till today "*Mere Sone Jaisa School Tum Logon ko Jail Lagta hai.*" (My golden School looks like a jail to you people.) Really it was a golden School as it gave us such precious memories that even today they are as fresh as they happened yesterday.

Mishra Sir was done with his killings and returned to his seat to write a note in our diaries I looked at Pappi and he looked at me and we both felt like laughing at this statement and were in fact laughing or rather trying to control our laughs as Rana and Upadhyay looked at us even they were laughing. Today when we look back we wonder how anyone could laugh so much after getting so severely thrashed up by the Principal.

He said to us, "This was your first time so I'm leaving you, but the next time you run from School and you are thrown out from this institution. You understand." We promised.

As we were led out of the Principal's den we were instructed by Binu Jacob to go to our classroom. After we were left alone to go to our classroom I said, "Oh my goodness my jaw is paining like hell. Fuck I took bloody fifty blows and you guys didn't get even a quarter of that and that Gattu Mishra I will kill that bloody asshole if I find him somewhere else other than School." That was the first GR or General Ragging of me in my life. As we moved through the corridor and reached our class, in the class beside ours Rekha was seated at her usual seat and she looked at me. This time there was a bit of sympathy in her eyes, she definitely had seen us running towards the wall, and maybe she had also come to know that five commandos from the neighbouring class had been taken prisoners of war and I was one of them and the whole School knew about the killer nature of the Principal towards these prisoners of war. I saw sympathy in her eyes.

As we entered the classroom it seemed that the whole class was laughing on us for getting caught in action. I felt so embarrassed. Not because we ran from School but because we got caught and that too for two silly and stupid reasons. The class was even laughing at us for being so stupid to get ourselves caught by two such professors who were thought to be the most lethargic characters in the School.

We took our seats at the last row. Binu Jacob came into the class and re took the attendance this time another of our classmate Swaroop Dutta was found to be missing from School. We thought he is dead tomorrow like us. For the remaining duration of the lecture we just kept quiet and after the Chemistry class was over we went to the drinking water bay where I met my brother, he said, *"Bhai* (brother) how can you be this silly to get caught by Binu Jacob and Gattu Mishra." This was more humiliation.

Soon it was lunch and all this time we sat in the Classroom dejected by the whole incident.

I said, "Enough is enough, and I can't take this humiliation anymore."

Pappi looked at me and said, "Me too." Rana and Upadhyay nodded with him.

I said, "Fine then lets take it out." We went out of the Classroom and headed towards our laboratories as we reached the laboratories we looked outside. There was no guard near the fenced wall from where we did our first adventure trip, I made my sprint followed by Pappi, Rana and Upadhyay and we all once again were outside the boundaries of our School, went straight to the woods where we changed our shirts and then went to the local tapri and bought four *WILLS NAVY CUTS* and as we lit them I looked at Pappi and said, "*Mera Sone Jaisa School Tum Logon ko Jail Lagta hai*" all of us broke into laughter and we enjoyed the day visiting various tableaux's.

6

JAI AND VEERU

Relive The Story

By the time festival season was over Pappi had quit Kajal coaching and joined Anil Coaching with Abhishek and Rohit aka Mausa, because his father wanted him to. The tutor Anil Gupta was friendly to Pappi and gang and always said, "Dude if you like any girl let me know I will introduce you to that girl and then you can take off from there."

There were two girls at the institute one of them was Sheetal and the other was Nidhi both of them studied in St. Theresa the same School in which Rinki and Arti used to study. Nidhi was a girl with the Miss India attitude. Once it happened that Nidhi got frustrated as Rohit asked too many questions and said, "*Rohit tumhari tube light der se jalti hai kya?"* (Rohit your brain works like a tube light). Rohit was in his own world so he didn't pay attention to it, but Pappi did and so did everyone else but nobody told Rohit as he lost temper very soon.

Now another angle to the whole scenario was that Pappi had fallen for Sheetal. Pappi knew that if Nidhi is not around then he will get a chance to be close to Sheetal. Well Sheetal was indeed a very beautiful girl and for Pappi one of the most beautiful girls he had ever seen in his entire life which obviously became the reason for Pappi to fall for her and this was not uncommon that Pappi did not fall for any girl he saw or who behaved nice with him. I thought that he is such a Jackass, where the bloody hell will he land up if he continues this way, well may be the answer is this book UNTITLED.

That day when the 'tube light' incident happened I met Pappi in the evening and he told me everything about the incidence while having our regular and Pappi was smoking it in style to be more precise like an underworld don of course inspired by SRK.

After he finished I could read his mind quite clearly that he had fallen for Sheetal. I said, "Why do you do all the time keep falling for one girl or the other, don't you understand that these things will not get you anywhere."

"*Bhai* I just want to talk to her and be friends with her and see if I have really fallen for her."

"Oye tharki (you pervert), I know that you are a jackass but why don't you realize that you are a jackass"

He gave me that 'Please do something' look.

I said, "This time you better settle down with Sheetal or else I am going to spank you with a whip. Now what is it that you want?"

"I need a chance to make an impression in her eyes, but with Nidhi, Abhishek and Mausa around I am not able to do that."

I took the *WILLS NAVY CUT* from him took a deep drag and said, "Well in that case these guys will give you that opportunity you are looking for."

"How come?"

"Well use your damned stinking political brain start playing with it dude."

"What is that supposed to mean?"

"Okay you Jackass with a dumb brain, listen, as you say whatever happened Mausa did not listen to it, so now Mausa will hear it."

"But how? And what will happen if Mausa listens to it?"

"You tell Mausa and that too make it sound as an insult being done to him, so that he takes immediate action on it."

"Fine then?"

"Then? What has happened to you idiot, is this *aashiqui* (love business) fucked your brains out. The rest will be like an automatic weapon; just load the magazine and pull the trigger."

Next day outside the class Pappi did exactly as I told him to do. He even added, "Arre if it had been me I would have shown her what is being a tube light then and there."

Rohit said, *"Tujha Aila,* did really she said all that about me."

"Yes my dear brother yes and I am really upset about this." Hearing these words Rohit's face went flaming red with anger, "I am going to show that bloody bitch who is a 'tube light'."

He went straight to Nidhi, "You bloody fucking bitch, how you dare call me a 'tube light'. What the fuck do you think of yourself? Next time you say something like this and I'm going to shove up your ass a real 'tube light'." By the time Rohit had finished his glorious lecture to Nidhi, she was already in shock and in tears. Sheetal who was standing right next to her was also in shock. Pappi headed straight to them and Abhishek followed him. Pappi began his glorious SRK act of pretending to stop Mausa from abusing Nidhi. Pappi said, “Rohit stop abusing her in public.” Hearing this Rohit’s temper again rose up and he yelled a few more abuses in hindi to Nidhi. Abhishek also got carried by Rohit and said, “Nidhi you shouldn’t have said that to Rohit infront of the whole class, it’s entirely your fault.”

Pappi said, “What’s wrong with you guys, now get over it and Abhishek you don’t start. Take Rohit inside the classroom.” Abhishek then took Rohit inside the classroom which by now was already vacant as the previous batch had left. Pappi turned to Nidhi and Sheetal and said, “I’m sorry on his behalf and ask forgiveness for them, I assure you that either of them will not ever say a single word to you in future and I guarantee that, so please forgive.” As Pappi said this in his usual SRK enactment Sheetal’s eyes saw an admiration for Pappi.

The plan had worked and now Pappi had an admiration for himself in Sheetal’s heart. After that day Nidhi quit the coaching and Sheetal was left alone in the class. It was not that tough for Pappi to keep away from Abhishek and Rohit while Sheetal was around. Their talks started and gradually the time span of their talks also increased from minutes to hours.

Pappi didn't have anything to do that afternoon so he reached the coaching a full hour before the scheduled time. The classroom was on second floor and had a balcony. Pappi was enjoying the view from that balcony, when he got the best view of life. Sheetal was dressed in a tight top revealing full access view for Pappi with an elegant long skirt. As Sheetal came in Pappi said, “Hi”

“Hi,” Sheetal replied

“Pretty early for tuition”

“Same for you”

“Well I didn't have anything to do so came; come lets take the front row seats.” Pappi said affirmatively. They took the first row seats. Silence came into the picture. Pappi looked at Sheetal passionately and said, “Sorry Sheetal.”

“Please Aayush don't embarrass me, it was Nidhi's fault.” Pappi took her beautiful face in his palm and turned her towards him and looked into her eyes with deep masculine essence. Their faces were so close to each other that Sheetal could feel his warm breath on her cheeks. As he moved forward to kiss her cheeks she turned to him and their lips felt each other. Sheetal made no attempt to release the lock. Pappi embraced her in his arms. He felt her skin between her tight top and long skirt. As he moved his hand up her top, she kissed him more forcefully and more passionately. The warmth of her skin made Pappi feel the feeling of love to the epitome. The globes of passion in Sheetal made Pappi feel like on top of the world. TAP THAK! TAP THAK! Some one was climbing the stairs of the coaching. Sheetal and Pappi quickly released the grip of love and adjusted their clothes as Anil Sir came in and said, "Hello People."

Year 1999 was the year of *Kuch Kuch Hota Hai* Shahrukh's movie and Pappi being his most ardent fan wanted to watch it but this time not with friends but with Sheetal to experience the love wave of the year's most successful romantic movie. The s-day well Sheeetal and Shahrukh day came and Pappi merely wished for the corner seats and the wish was granted.

The show was in Raj Cinema, a newly constructed theatre with Digital sound and comfortable leather seats. Well comfortable for an intimate show of romantic movie for a couple, good show for the other audiences. By the time the movie reached interval Pappi was full on for an intimate romantic session with Sheetal, but Pappi lived in Bhopal and the movie theatre he went to was full of crowd commonly known as '*Bhopalis*', who during a movie deliver more dialogues than the actors themselves and these dialogues come in form of 'hooting' and if these *Bhopalis* could see another intimate show in the same theatre absolutely free of cost, they would leave no dialogue unturned to make it harassing to death for Sheetal and Pappi. Pappi couldn't control him from getting intimate with Sheetal but the fear of these *Bhopalis* kept him from making a move, result was very very frustrated Pappi by the end of movie.

Once out of the movie hall Sheetal could clearly see a frustrated and depressed Pappi, she suggested coffee to make his mood better. In the coffee shop Sheetal said, "I have heard about Raman School that the boys bunk classes and run out of School, Are you one of them?"

"Yes"

"Where do you go from the School?"

"Sometimes movies sometimes to nearby woods."

"Sounds fun."

"Yes it is, would you like to experience the woods."

"Yes."

Pappi took her to the woods, they sat under a tree. It was very romantic for Pappi he started imagining the scene from Silsila movie '*Yeh kahan aa gaye hum*'.

"Are you depressed?" Sheetal asked him

"No just angry"

“Reason?”

“Those bastards in the movie hall”.

“Ohh, forget them”.

Sheetal kissed him on forehead. Pappi put his head on her lap.

“I Love You”.

“Love you too” Sheetal answered

“Don’t you think this is a romantic evening and location?”

“Yes”

“Pappi what’s the difference between love and romance?”

This question gave Pappi the chance to fulfil his desire of being intimate with Sheetal.

“Love and romance are very different in ways of expression”

“How?” Sheetal asked very keenly.

“When we love someone above the lips it is called love.”

“And what is romance?”

“When we kiss and love someone below lips it is romance”

"Can you explain?”

Pappi held her face kissed her on cheek, “this is love”.

Then he kissed her lips, "this is also love".

Sheetal was enjoying this intimacy of youth. Then he kissed her neck "this is romance".

And slowly he kissed all of her body. Sheetal had the body of a Goddess and her fair glowy and shiny skin made Pappi's evening even more memorable.

The fateful day: One day when Sheetal was going home and as usual Pappi behind her suddenly a boy came and tried to talk to her. She started crying while this boy was talking to her. Pappi was surprised, he raced towards her. As the boy saw Pappi coming, left her and sped away on his bike. Pappi asked Sheetal "Who is he?"

"I don't know who is he but he is chasing me everyday and is disturbing me."

"Please don't cry and go home the next time he shows up I will teach him a lesson."

"No leave him, there are lot of guys like this and with how many can you pick up a fight, leave it." Pappi that day realized that Sheetal had also developed some liking for him.

The next few days Pappi didn't follow Sheetal. Then one day Sheetal said to Pappi, "Can you please come with me till my home."

"Why? Is everything alright?"

"That guy is bothering me too much; he is following me everyday, save me from harm Aayush please."

Pappi immediately gave me a call and informed me of the situation. I reached his coaching around 5 minutes before the scheduled time when his class got over and waited for him. They came out and Sheetal went in the mini–bus. We followed that bus on my *Hero Puch* (a moped available in the 90s) till *Bijli colony*. I parked my Hero Puch at a sweet shop and followed her. All of a sudden that guy came and forced Sheetal to sit on his bike but she refused. This was the moment when Pappi's patience was over the limit. We raced towards Sheetal and WHACK! Pappi slapped the guy on his face, the force must have been equal to '5G' force and the drama started. The guy was furious and was about to hit Pappi when I stepped in. I held him and said, "*Boss kyun haddi tudwana chahta hai?*

(Dude why do you want to get broken bones) You better get out of here."

He said, "You two stay here only I will be back right away and then show *kaun kiski haddi todta hai* (who will break who's bones), just stay here."

As he went Sheetal started screaming and said, "You guys run away from here or else you might be in trouble. You don't know him; he is Thomas and is a goon here."

I said, "Pappi you escort her safely to her home and I will wait for you here."

Pappi said, "No I will stay with you. Sheetal you run and go home." Suddenly we saw 8-10 guys coming towards us along with Thomas, we had couple of our friends staying in Bijli colony, but there was no time to call for rescue. I yelled at Pappi, "Idiot try and understand if all three of us run then its easy for them to catch us as Sheetal will not be able to run as fast as us and then all three of us will be in big trouble, I will stop them here, this will buy you both time to make it to Sheetal's home by that time and don't worry I will be alright, now go run!"

But Pappi was not ready to leave me alone and said, "No I cannot."

"Don't be silly, try and understand, please go, please go."

"What the hell do you think of yourself? You can alone take on 8-10 guys by yourself; no I can't let that happen to you."

"I know I can't take them alone, but it's the matter of your safety and Sheetal's safety I may not be able to stop them for long but I can surely stop for at least few extra minutes which would be enough for both you to get to safety." But Pappi being a true friend was not ready to leave me at any cost, it didn't matter whether the cost would be danger to Sheetal all that mattered was *his best friend*. At last seeing that the enemy had already advanced very near to us, I made him *swear on our friendship* to run and with tears in his eyes Pappi headed off with Sheetal leaving his best friend.

Those guys came up to me I was preparing myself for the battle which was about to begin. I knew it was going to be a physical one and I was outnumbered 10 to 1, but I decided no matter what I will knock down at least Thomas and more importantly no one gets to reach to Pappi, I slowly took out my belt. As Thomas swung his hand and hit me on my neck I swung my belt and hit him hard on the forehead with the buckle of the belt. Thomas was knocked out. The other 9 guys pounced on me with chains, stumps and what not. They were too much for me to handle alone. I was hit in the face, ribs, backbone, and nose and was bleeding. I fell on the ground and kept lying there till the guys got tired of kicking me and hitting me. They thought that I was unconscious and I heard Thomas say that, "C'mon this asshole is dead now lets find out Sheetal" I kept lying as I didn't have the energy left in my body to get up.

Pappi quickly dropped Sheetal at her home and then hurried back to me with four of our friends staying in the area, but everything was over by then.

Pappi saw me lying on the road bleeding, he took me in his laps gave me water and said sorry a million times to have left me in this situation. I said, “I didn’t let them touch you *bhai*.”

Pappi was filled with tears, “I will never ever leave you alone again.”

“I told you dude for these crushes of yours I will get kicked in my butt and then it becomes a pain in the ass, see it has come true.” Pappi cried and at the same time he smiled.

He took me to the hospital. There I told him, “I knocked out Thomas but they were huge in numbers, for sometime I fought them but then realizing that there was no point in fighting so many guys and you and Sheetal must have been safe by now, so its better to lie down and pretend to be unconscious.” Pappi realized that not just him even I was also a very good actor. This whole incident reminded Pappi of the movie Sholay and as both of us had our favourite song of that movie *"Yeh Dosti Hum Nahi Todenge"* (we will not break our friendship). It was true it further strengthened our friendship to withstand every pressure of life and be with each other in all thick and thin of life. Pappi started calling me *Jai pra* (Jai bro) after the name of the character which the legendary *Amitabh Bachchan* played and died saving his friend. The character of friend which was played by the legendary *Dharmendra* and I started called him *Veeru pra* (Veeru Bro) after the name of the character played by Dharmendra.

Readers you might be wondering what happened to Sheetal. Well Pappi was fooled once again in love. Pappi thought she will come to say thanks to him for doing all this but that didn't happened which put a big question in Pappi's mind. After two days of that incident Pappi went to see Sheetal at her home but was shocked by whatever he saw. Sheetal was with Thomas and both were laughing and were having good time. This confused Pappi and on enquiring Pappi came to knew that Thomas was her boyfriend and some miscreants had created misunderstanding between them as they both explained Pappi about it everything became clear.

When Pappi told me about the facts I thought what a drama. I got hit because of somebody else's girlfriend. The thought of Sheetal making use of Pappi to get rid of Thomas even more infuriated me, I was really mad with anger and I said to Pappi, "Buddy let's go we need to take revenge on Thomas and Sheetal and everyone involved in this, I will fucking beat the hell out of that dog Thomas."

"No yaar leave the two love birds alone it was not their fault they were the victims of misunderstanding created by some enemies of Thomas, but yes we will revenge your fight with those other 9 fellows also I don't want to see Sheetal in pain."

"*Tu saala* (You bloody), you will not give up being senti on girls, okay but we will revenge those nine fellows who were with Thomas that day." After that we slammed the nine friends of Thomas and took a revenge on them.

Few days later Pappi said in a very depressed tone, "I am fooled again in love. But what can I do, anybody would have been fooled in this situation." I started laughing at him, "Not everybody my dear aashiq only you are a fool. You are born to be fooled by the girls' innocence you Jackass."

Sheetal left Anil coaching and all efforts by Pappi were wasted but this incident made us realize what living and dying for a friend is, what great pleasure it is to not even think once about giving your life for your best friend and it makes you feel on top of the world when you know that there is one person on this planet with whom you can even trust your life. Long live friendship. After this incidence Pappi promised to himself that he will never get into this kind of situation ever again, but as always....

Promises are meant to be broken....

7

MY PHYSICS TEACHER

With November came the test season, and it was time for our unit tests which was supposed to be the preparation tests for our 2nd terminal examinations which were due to be held in December. Normally my gang and I didn't bother about these unit tests but that day was different. We couldn't escape out of School due to whole day surveillance at all the escape points and we were forced to attend the second half of School. To our surprise the physics lecture turned to be a unit test. I was quite comfortable with that as I was under the impression that our class teacher Mr. Binu Jacob would be conducting the test and the syllabus would consist of Applied Mechanics. I was quite good in Applied Mechanics so I didn't see any reason to worry. But after a few minutes I saw the reason to worry.

Another physics teacher named *Deepa Verma* entered our class. Deepa Verma was a very beautiful looking lady must have been in her mid–twenties and was indeed very beautiful, some even said that she used to work as an Air–Hostess but after her marriage she quit that job and became a physics teacher.

Her subject was ray-optics and I was not very good at that subject. When she entered the class the whole class which was a fish market few seconds ago fell all silent, not because a teacher entered the class but because a beautiful young lady had entered the class and the already mal–nourished class (in terms of beautiful faces) just felt like it was an invitation to get some green tonic for their eyes, and everyone was just gazing at her, obviously not listening to her instructions for the test. For the test I sat with Rana. Pappi took the seat on the desk besides me with Abhishek. As the test began Deepa Verma wrote the five questions for the test on the blackboard, all the questions seemed to me as alien questions and I had never heard of it. One question had numerical values of refractive indexes of three different types of glasses and we had to find out the final angle by which the ray of light would bend after coming out of the third glass piece. Another question was to derive some ray–optics equation to prove that light bends more in glass than in water. All those questions were something of which I had never heard of. I wondered what could I do, then I looked at Pappi who was looking even more confused and frustrated, I knew that there was no point asking him just then realized that Rana had not surrendered his copy of physics book and we could copy the answers for at least two questions.

I said, "Rana, take out the book."

"Which book?"

"The physics book you dumbass take it out." Rana took out the physics book from his bag. Now all I had to do was to go the chapter in ray–optics and find out the derivation in the book and then just copy it. I started searching the book for the derivation even Rana was looking for it. We found the derivation. There were two of them identical, and it started a debate between us as to which one was being asked in the question as the debate continued Rana said, "*Bhai* I know this is the one it, I remember it." I saw no point in continuing this debate so I agreed to Rana and said, "Fine, but you better make sure that this is it or else I am going to break your neck like this." As I said this I held his neck with my hands, in all this I completely forgot that Deepa Verma was still in the class, she was at the door talking to some other teacher, just then she turned around and saw me squeezing Rana's neck. Oh! fuck I was dead, she came walking quickly towards us and asked me "What were you doing right now?"

"Nothing ma'am"

"No I saw you beating Rana. Tell me why were you beating him?"

"No ma'am I was not beating him. He is my cousin why should I beat him?"

She then asked Rana, "He was beating you and squeezing your neck I saw it, tell me the truth and I will get him punished."

"No ma'am absolutely no, he did not even touch me, you must have mistaken."

"See even he confirms it." These two replies made Deepa Verma even more furious. I must admit that she looked even more gorgeous when she was angry. The whole class was looking at us. She said, "You guys are creating nuisance in the class and disturbing the class." As she finished her statement she swung her left hand towards me. As her hand came with reflex action I held her hand in air. Now I was holding her hand and she was growing red and hot with anger. Wow! She was hot. I mean while holding her hand I could feel that her body temperature was quite high and of course her hands were very soft. With a jerk she pulled out her hand from mine and went out of the class quickly. It now became a hot subject, every single boy came to me and asked, “Wow man you held her hand, how did it feel?”

I just said, “Hot.”

At the back of my mind I knew that this is not just the end of it, such things don’t leave you so easily. No later than 5 minutes after Deepa Verma left the classroom I saw Binu Jacob entering the classroom, the entire classroom felt silent. “Anupam, come out I need to talk to you.” I recalled that thrashing of me by the Principal Mishra Sir, my jaw structure started to pain, but I decided to be brave and went out. As I went out Binu Sir said, “What did you do?”

“Nothing Sir.”

“Now Anupam tell me the truth, Deepa Verma just came out of the classroom in tears and she is in the staff room sitting in very upset mood and with moist eyes.”

“Nothing sir, I did nothing.”

“Look Anupam I know there is something which you have done as when I asked her she just took your name and was weeping and she said to me to ask you, now tell me what it is?”

“Actually sir today there was this unit test thing and I did not know that it was a ray–optics test and I was not prepared for it, so just asked Rana an answer and she thought that I was fighting with him and got furious. I told her that there was nothing of this sort but she did not agree. Even Rana and Aayush told her that we were not fighting. But she did not believe and she raised her hand to hit me, I just stopped her from hitting me by blocking her hand. That is the whole story sir." Binu Jacob then thought for a moment and said, "Hmmm, but Anupam you shouldn't have held her hand."

"Sir I did not hold her hand with any bad intention. I was defending myself, and I don't agree that for such a reason a lady should raise her hand."

"Yes I understand, but then the issue is a bit serious we need to do something about it."

"Fine sir then I will go and say sorry to Deepa madam."

"Okay next time when you see her then say sorry. I will talk to her and try to get things in control."

Hearing this I was relieved and thought may be things won't be that bad this time and surprisingly Binu Jacob had been successful in persuading Deepa Verma that it was nothing intentional and I tried to just defend myself and also he was able to convince her that raising hands on guys who are in 11th standard and are grown ups is not a good thing for a lady teacher and such incidents or worse can happen. She saw his point in saying it. Next day when I saw Deepa Verma I went up to her and said, “Ma’am I am sorry for whatever happened yesterday and I did not do it intentionally, it was just by my reflex action that it happened.”

“Okay Anupam I forgive you, but you should learn to respect your teachers more.”

“Yes ma’am.”

“Okay you can go now.” That was probably one of the rarest of the episodes in my life where I escaped big trouble by the margin of hair. But this incident made me quite famous in School the word spread rapidly across the School and soon everyone came to me to ask ‘hey are you the guy who had held Deepa Verma’s hand in front of the whole classroom’ these versions of the story were sounded more like that I held her hand like a hero does with a heroine in a Bollywood movie while romancing with her. I even heard one modified script of the story as ‘Anupam held Deepa Verma’s hand in front of the whole class and proposed to her and that’s why she went out of the class with tears in her eyes’ all these sounded ridiculous to me, but again there was nothing much I could do for it, I just hoped that these kinds of news didn’t reach Rekha’s ears, well although I was in Love with that girl from Convent School but then again who wants to have a bad impression in the eyes of a beautiful girl like Rekha and that too because of some story which has not at all occurred, well at least the distorted versions were a complete lie.

8

SCHOOL OF DREAMS

RAMAN - PART 2

Soon the academic session got over in 11th and it was time for our annual exams. The annual exams time table was released. For Pappi the only reason to worry was that this time in our School the results were going to be a combined result of 1st term, 2nd term and finals. Although he had cleared the 1st and 2nd terminal but his marks in Chemistry were very less and like most of good science students or budding engineers he was very weak in Chemistry. For me the only worry was my impression on teachers. After all the running away from School incidents and holding the physics teacher's hand infront of the whole class had successfully managed to get me into the hit-list for class 11th 'C' and the worry was that although the exam paper's would be set by the board but the answer sheets would be checked in School itself and with that impression I could think of the worst nightmare as failing in the annual exams.

But our case was not applicable on Rana or Ravi as both of them had left concentrating on their studies a lot earlier. Their most of the time was spent in just roaming around.

The papers were tough, even though they were from MP Board. The Chemistry paper as expected made us panic and burn the midnight oil.

The day when the results were to be announced came. It was required to come along with some guardian to take the result. I went there with my Dad. As I entered the classroom Binu Sir was seated there handing out results to some of my classmates. As he saw me he said, "Ah Anupam come come." I wished him and introduced him to my Dad. After the introductions My Dad asked, "Sir what is his result?" Binu took out my report card and said, "Don't worry Sir he has done well and got good marks and have been promoted to 12th." My Dad was quite happy to hear that and I was relieved to hear that. Binu said, "Anupam try to perform better in Chemistry. Your marks in Physics and Mathematics are good but for MPPET (Madhya Pradesh Pre Engineering Test) you need to improve on Chemistry." I nodded my head. My Dad said, "Okay, thank you so much sir, now we shall leave."

Binu said, "Yes sir, but Anupam could you wait a bit I need to talk to you."

My Dad said, "Is everything alright sir?"

"Everything is fine sir, just wanted to talk to him about his (Pre Engineering Test) (PET) preparations."

Binu said, "Anupam you are good student you scored faboulous in Physics, in fact you have scored 3rd highest marks in Physics in School. Also you have performed well in Mathematics."

"Thank you Sir"

"Anupam you are PET or IIT material why do you move around with Rana he is not a good boy."

I said, "Sir he is my cousin and we have family relations so I cannot stop being with him completely."

"I understand your situation but then try to stay away from him as far as possible. By the way did you know Rana has failed in Physics and Chemistry?" Now that was a bomb explosion. Then Binu said, "I have already given him grace marks and promoted him to 12th standard but Ravi has failed and he will be expelled from the School. Prepare well for your competitive exams and try to keep away from Ranadeb, he will do you no good." I nodded my head in agreement.

For Pappi as there was construction work going at Pappi's home so his father asked him go along with any elder from neighbourhood. He took Raju along with him. Raju was 3-4 years older to him and they had been playing cricket together in the neighbourhood since long so they had become good friends.

They entered in the School in his *neeli khataara* (blue broken) scooter Priya. Ravi was standing at the gate with his father. He told Pappi that he has failed.

Prashant Channe was also standing there and he had also failed but he gave another shocking news that Abhishek Singh had also failed but his mom was an ex teacher of Radhakrishnan and vice Principal Mandloi madam knew his mom so Abhishek was promoted to 12th class but she also told them to leave as soon as possible because if other students knew this then it will become a problem.

As Pappi went to the classroom where Binu Jacob was sitting on the way he met 3–4 more of friends and some of them got supplementary and some of them failed. His mind was now a mixed bag of fear, agony and trauma, suddenly he realized someone tapping his shoulder. He turned around to see me smiling behind him. I said to him, "Hey dude why are you worrying so much? Don't worry dude both of us will attend the 12th standard classes together." Raju was also trying to comfort him by giving him support and courage. As they went inside the classroom Pappi wished Binu sir and after the usual exchange of greetings Binu took off his specs and said, *"haan Aayush kya haal hai?"* (Yes, Aayush how are you?)

"Not good sir." Binu again put on his specs looked at Raju and Pappi with a questioning face. Pappi said, "He is my elder brother sir."

"Okay." Then he continued, "Here is your result Aayush, hmmmm, you have passed and have been promoted to class 12th but I had to request Ameen Sir to give grace marks to you, because you had failed in Chemistry by three marks. I convinced him that you are a good student and you will do better in future." These words fell on Pappi's ears like some soothing romantic song being sung by Rinki. He fell on the feets of Binu sir touched them and said, "Thank you so much sir." Even Binu was moved by this and he said, "No problem, but you must thank Ameen Sir"

After reaching home where Raju said to Pappi's Dad, "Uncle your son has passed and has been promoted to class 12th and he has scored the 4th rank in class." Pappi's Dad was too happy to hear this also that day was a day for double celebration as the second floor slab of his house was completed successfully. So his Dad gave everyone a treat with sweets and samosas.

After that once again Pappi made another promise to himself that he will keep everybody's words and will work harder on his studies.

But for him promises are meant to be broken....

9

SCHOOL OF DREAMS

RAMAN -PART 3

For me the pressure was on for cracking the entrance exams and get into the IITs or (Regional Engineering College) (RECs). I applied for admission to Joe's classes one of the best for competitive exam preparation, but I was not selected because I didn't perform up to mark in the admission test which was on complex numbers. Those numbers were really complex for my simple brain, which would collapse under the complexities of the symbol 'i' called iota. I could never really understand the underroot function of-1. The general equation of complex number 'a+bi' was so complex for me that I couldn't understand why didn't c come after a and b. To add to it was the concept where a and b were called real numbers and 'i' was an imaginery number. Never in my life was I taught to imagine number.

After a few days my old friends from St. Xavier's Deven and Vipin came to my home. During our talks they told me that another famous coaching institute 'S' classes was going to start its fresh 12th standard batch for IIT/JEE from next week and there would be no admission test. I thought of giving it a try.

As I entered the classroom which was a big hall on the top floor of a 3 storied building and there were chairs arranged neatly into rows with a passage in the middle. Later I realized that they were two separate seating arrangements for boys and girls. I took the isle seat.

After me and my friends took our seats sir came in and said, "Anek, how are you? Kya kar rahe ho? How do you feel for this new batch?" Then he looked at me and said, "Hey new face. What's your name?"

"Hello sir, I'm Anupam and this is my first time in your class." He pointed at Anek and said, "Welcome. Are you his friend?"

"Yes Sir."

"Very good. We will start the class in 10 minutes" And went out of the classroom.

After he went out we started our chit chat and by this time a few girls had also entered the class. After almost 10 minutes a girl entered with two of her friends as I looked at her my eyes couldn't believe the sight. My brain went for a 360 degree negative G dive and I went numb completely, for the next several seconds my eyes were fixed on that face I kept staring at the most beautiful face in the world. Wondering was it a dream or was it real, I saw the girl with whom I fell in love at first sight at a traffic signal. She saw me staring at her without even blinking my eyes once; she gave me an astonished look as if saying "What?" I just loved that look of her's. She took her seat I could almost stretch out my arm and touch her beautiful hair. Everything about her was perfect she was the most perfect girl I had ever seen in my life. It was only when sir entered I realized that I was in a coaching class. The next two hours I spent just looking at her, all the other guys saw me admiring the most beautiful girl in my life and laughed at me. I was as well quite conscious of sir as I didn't want to get kicked out of the institute on the very first day because of my staring at the most beautiful girl in the world. Well the reason was not that I would miss out to be a part of one of the best classes in the city but I didn't want to lose the opportunity to be close to her for six days a week, 2-3 hours everyday and for the whole year. I just loved her.

That night I didn't sleep once again, her face just didn't go off my eyes. I remembered the future prediction done by that good spirit the first time I did Planchette. Once again it made me wonder how the prediction can be so accurate but it was.

The next day I called up Pappi and said, "Pappi I am going to join S's classes."

"Really, even I am going to join the same."

"Wow great, which batch are you joining?"

"The one which starts at 5.45."

"Wow me too joining the same batch."

"That's great news buddy, so then you come to my home every morning and then we go together to the class."

I said, "But why should I come, I think it will be better if you come to my place and then we go to M.P.Nagar and why should I come to your home early in the morning, the batch is in evening."

"No the batch timings are 5.45 A.M that's morning and the classes are in Indrapuri not M.P.Nagar."

"Hang on dude, wait a moment, which classes are you talking about."

"Shukla classes for MPPET 5.45 A.M, the morning batch for 12th standard students." I then realized that he was going for MPPET batches and I had taken up the IIT/JEE classes. I said, "Ohh dude

I was talking about the IIT/JEE classes batch held in evening at 5.45 P.M at M.P.Nagar. You aren't joining the IIT/JEE classes."

"Na baba, MPPET is good enough for me, IIT/JEE is not my cup of tea."

"Fine dude, but I will not be leaving these IIT classes in any case."

Pappi sensed the excitement in my tone and asked, "What is it?"

"Yaar, she is coming to the same classes."

"Who? That love at first sight girl of yours?"

"Yes!"

"Unbelievable dude! You wait I'm coming over, then we will talk."

Those summers were the best summers of my life, the most beautiful face for eyes was infront of my eyes, I could see her daily Monday to Sunday everyday and that made those summers the coolest summers of my life.

One fine Sunday in the class Shukla sir gave us a rapid fire test on mechanics to do. He knew I was quite good at mechanics so he expected me to complete the test with accuracy in the given time, but my only concentration was that lovely face. I was seated at my usual isle seat and she was seated right besides me on the isle seat of the girl's section. Even though I started solving the questions but only with half mind, after the stipulated one hour sir came back and said, “Show me your answers.” Of the twenty questions I managed only fifteen. Shukla sir said, “*Anupam kya kar raha tha*? Only fifteen questions solved.”

“Sir the questions were tough.” He gave me ‘no fooling around me’ look and said, “Okay, let’s check out the answers.” One by one he started solving the questions on the white board; he would ask each one of us for the answer. On one question which was relatively an easier question and should have been solved within a minute, I did it but made a silly calculation mistake so the final answer was obviously wrong. As I declared my answer Shukla sir came up to me and said, “Show me your solution.”

I showed him my notebook and he took a quick glance at it and said, “Well Anupam Ji, what is the -1 x -1?”

“1”

“So why is it -1 here?” I looked at thc solution and grinned. He hit four punches on my back like an elder brother, when I saw that girl’s face, she was looking at me getting hit by sir with her one eyelid closed and her face had an expression which had empathy for me, but she was looking really cute with her one eye lid closed. Sir said, “*Kya kar raha tha tu*? (What were you doing?)

This way it won't work Anupam you need to concentrate hard."

"Yes sir." He then turned to that girl and said, "*Yes Miss Abhishikta ji aapka answer kya hai?* (Yes, Miss Abhishikta, what is your answer?)" 'Whoa! So that's her name' I thought, I had heard the name for the first time. Even her answer was wrong. Shukla sir then returned back to the white board and said, "What has been happening to you guys? Why are you guys not concentrating hard enough?" He gave me a look which said 'No Chasing Girls' I nodded. But then I was not to listen to him and risk my career for the most precious thing of my life Abhishikta. That was the first step towards making my own life UNTITLED. My concentration levels in studies had really gone down and my love for Abhishikta kept going like a soaring space shuttle which even today is flying high.

As the days passed my summer vacations ended and it was a new beginning for all of us. The class of 11th 'C' was re-named as the class of 12th 'B'. Well it was a co-incidence that we became part of the most renowned section of Raman, the glorious past of which was stated by the vigour and glamour of my elder brother's batch. It was their pioneering batch which had made the section famous and brought it successfully to the top of the chart or the so-called hit-list of Raman School.

Their gallant efforts of mass bunking of classes after lunch and optimize the utilization of proxy attendance made them so famous that their classroom was shifted from the farthest corner of the School to the classroom right infront of the Principal's room.

When 11th 'C' was allotted the section 12th 'B' there was additional pressure on the class teacher Mrs. Alka Pandya for keeping this section of intelligent and impish devils under control. Alka madam was a motherly figure to all of us, not just to all of us but to the previous batch as well. She was a sweet lady with a PhD in Chemistry and an excellent teacher. All her previous students respected her very much. She pretended to be strict with everyone who escaped School but deep inside somewhere may be she knew that a lot of these guys would bring laurel and glory of MPPET and IIT/JEE selections for her.

Our group got this class but the only guy that was missing was Ravi. He had failed so he had been rusticated from the School, even after that he was a part of our group courtesy Rana and Abhishek. At times he used to ask Pappi, "What should I do yaar?" Pappi although not very happy with him because he was up to playing tricks against me but still being a helpful guy advised him to appear for the class 12th exams by filling in the private candidate form. Ravi mentioned his financial problem of not being able to arrange money for his studies and coaching to Pappi. Pappi offered him Maths tuitions free of cost, this way he would be able to revise his concepts and Ravi would get free Maths tuitions and notes. All this while Pappi's friendship with Abhishek grew as in Pappi's words Abhishek became his fan.

Ravi used to be free the whole day; he never went to any School. He waited for Abhishek and Rana outside the School, as soon as both of them escaped from School Ravi met them at the nearby woods and then they went for movies. Most of the days it happened that Rana didn't even come inside the School campus. I even asked him to at least attend labs for practicals but he didn't pay any attention to that. Pappi and I attended the practical's, as teachers used to pay special attention to each and every student with practicals which was very important for the board exam practicals, these teachers would be the one to save our asses from the externals.

10

MUDDY ESCAPES

And Old Fractures

The month of July brought in showers and made the ceinate beautiful and the environment green. Everything looked so fresh and green but then it was all in bird's eye view. The actual ground showed a different picture which included long wet grass, muddy fields, water pools and buffaloes chilling out in those pools.

That was a Wednesday when Rana, Pappi, Abhishek and I went on our escape mission. Rana was the first one to reach the boundary wall as usual he tossed up his School bag high up in the Air and by the time he climbed up the wall we all could hear a big splash. I looked at Pappi, he shrugged and we continued the climb, by the time Rana lept off the wall I heard another big splash, this time the sound was even bigger, after that I heard another splash and then another, by this time I could hear Rana's voice at full scream saying, *"Mat phek, mat phek.* (Don't throw, Don't throw)" But by this time all our School bags were already floating in the water pool. Rana, Pappi and Abhishek were standing on the road with their trousers wet well above their knees, as I made my jump I tried to make it a long jump to avoid the deep waters, but my long jump skills were not good enough to make it safely across the wide sea of rain water, although I managed to pull off most part of the water but I landed on the last part where the water was less but the mud was abundant as I landed my right leg landed in water which was calf deep for me and my left leg slided on the muddy slope ruining the left part of my trouser with mud. Just then we saw another bag flying in the air, it landed with a splash just as we turned around we saw a body flying off the walls and the body landed with a large splash of water, after the water splash silenced off we saw the commerce boy lying on his back in the water pool with a buffalo regurgitating infront of his face. It seemed the buffalo didn't get moved at all by this action taking place in its vicinity. Later when we were in the nearby woods smoking our very old brand of *NAVY Cut* I said, "Oye why the hell didn't you warn us about the water pool outside the walls."

"What do you think, why was I shouting *mat pheko mat pheko*."

"Abey just by shouting *mat pheko* do you want us to understand what is going on?" Rana was frustrated.

Pappi said, "Its okay *yaar*, no problems, by the way that guy what a flyer he had today. Bloody it seemed like as if he would have half landed on that buffalo."

I said, "Yeah and looking at the buffalo it semmed like it wouldn't have mattered even if the guy had half landed on it, it was regurgitating its fodder with such ease and charm."

After that incident we became extra careful while escaping our way out from the School but as it is said one can never be extra careful and if that person is Pappi one needs to make extra efforts to be careful leave aside being extra careful.

That day after the 3rd lecture we shot off like bullets my run and Rana's run till the walls was perfect and the timing with which we crossed over the boundary was perfect, but as usual Pappi started his run with a delay, when he saw Paramlal following us he ran even harder, generating extra pace and extra kinetic energy. That extra kinetic energy was more than enough to make him cross the boundary but the whole of the kinetic energy didn't get converted into potential energy and when he fell off the wall. He landed on his right leg with the whole of his mass of his body on his right ankle. In the process he sprained his ankle which he had already sprained in a football match almost a year ago.

None of us realized that the sprain was of such intensity that he almost dislocated his ankle; the ligaments were no doubt torn. By the time he reached home his ankle was twice the normal size. Later on the pain became too much that he wasn't even able to come to School on his own. After that nasty landing Pappi had a plaster in his left leg due to which even walking was not possible for him. He spent a few days at home then he started coming to School. It was either Abhishek or I who had to go and pick him up for School.

All of us ran off from School and he had to attend classes, well how could this be tolerated by Pappi. One day he said to me, "Yaar I want to get out of School with you guys' attending the classes is getting too much on my nerves." I looked at him then his plastered leg and nodded. Then he said, "But yaar I have a plastered leg and I would need support to get out."

"Yeah even I was thinking about that. Don't worry we will work something around, I'm with you." Even Abhishek said the same thing, infact he was overen thusiatic about it and had said we will take you with us or no one goes.

After the 3rd lecture it was time to run to the wall and get out. After crossing the labs everyone spirinted off including Abhishek; as Pappi had a plaster on his leg he could not run but he was limping as fast as he could. All others reached the wall and no one of them even bothered to look behind what's happening to Pappi. Poor Pappi was left alone and stranded at that time limping his way across the field to the wall. Somehow he managed to reach the wall but with a plastered leg it was practically impossible for him to climb it on his own. In the meanwhile I went to the drinking water bay to have some water. When I reached the labs I saw Paramlal advancing towards the wall I could see the guys' climbing and jumping the wall. I started my spirint towards the wall, upon reaching the wall I saw Pappi dangling on the wall with two halves of his body on either side of the wall.

I said, *"bhanchod, abe tu andar aa raha hai ya bahar jaa raha hai"* (Are you coming in or going out). He turned around and saw me; I saw his frozen face with fear. The first time when we got caught he said he told the Principal that had fever so he ran off, now if he says that he had a broken leg and that's why he was running and that too by climbing a damned 10 foot high wall Mishra sir would have broken both his legs. I knew his fear and gave him a mighty push on his ass, with that push he got the required force to climb up the wall. By the time Paramlal reached the wall I took him out to safety. He then said, “Buddy how come you were late?”

“Actually I went to the drinking water bay, also I had feared what happened so I started off a bit late and by the time I came back I saw what I expected, you deserted by everyone and your ass dangling from the wall. So it was again on me to push your asses you fatso.” Pappi hearing this hugged me tight and said, “Buddy you once again saved my ass.”

We reached the place where our bikes were parked there we saw Abhishek and the others; Pappi rebuked Abhishek for leaving him mid–air and not caring for him. Abhishek said sorry a repeated number of times and Pappi in those days being a cool calm guy forgave him for his deeds. This incident further strengthened our bond, as we have always stood by each other. In the words of Pappi, “The friendship of Jai and Veeru will live forever.”

11

PAPPI THE SAVIOUR
OF 12th 'B'

We appeared for our first terminal exams in class 12th in the month of August. When the answer sheets were shown to the class and Pappi summed his marks of all the papers the total percentage stood at 71% but due to some mistake the class teacher gave him 41%. Pappi went to her and told her that his score is 71%, she said rudely, "How is it possible?" Pappi's impression story was a bit screwed up here due to the School bunking adventures and this made Alka madam think that he would not pass the exams. She calculated the marks again and found that Pappi was right, she looked at him smiled and said, "Good Aayush." After that her behaviour towards Pappi changed, slowly, he became one of her favourite students.

While teaching in class if she would ask are you guys' bored and don't want to study anymore. If Pappi said yes the she used to stop teaching, so it kind of validated his theory of being a favourable student. But being a favoured student also has its own disadvantages like for Pappi he had to attend most of the classes and could bunk only when it was safe with respect to Alka madam not noticing him. Of course he had an impression and reputation to protect.

Once it happened that after much speculation Pappi ran along with Abhishek, Rana and me from School. This time we took the same route on which we were caught while running from School almost a year ago. There used to be two trees on either side of the wall. That day a bull was having its afternoon lunch beneath the shade of the tree which was on the outerside of the wall. Pappi as usual being a lazy ass, was the last one to jump the wall. After jumping outside I shouted, "Pappi be careful, *neeche saand baitha hai* (There is a bull sitting right below)." But till that time he had already released his bum in air and was floating in air. When he landed he found himself on the back of that bull. Due to this sudden fall of Pappi's ass that weighted around 60Kgs, the Bull was shaken as if the whole sky had fallen upon him. The bull stood up with fear and ran away from there with fear. Although the bull looked quite ferocious but then no matter how ferocious a creature is, it has the fear of death and if you unladen somewhere close to fifty kilos of mass on the creature it is bound to scare the hell out of him. So the bull ran away. It was fun watching Pappi falling over a bull upon his ass. We all laughed till our stomach ached. I said, "*Pappi beta who saand teri gand laga deta* (Pappi, son that bull would have taken your butt apart). You were bloody lucky to get your ass not punctured by the horns of that bull. Had you fallen in front of him instead of over him, he would have played the Spanish bull fight with your ass." To this even Pappi laughed but the shiver of fear was clearly visible on his face, which went white with fear.

That day Alka madam came to know that almost all of the most notorious class had escaped the School once again so she came and took attendance.

The next day all of us decided to bunk School and not to go to School for some 2-3 days till the time matter gets into the cold bag.

That week we bunked the whole week and went back on Monday and thought that Pandya madam must have forgotten and now nothing will happen but how can any trouble bypass us so easily, as Alka madam started taking the roll call. Abhishek was the first roll number he answered yes to his roll call and madam said, "Keep standing, don't sit." She had a mark up of all the guys against their names who ran away from School that day.

Pandya madam targeted Pappi first as he was her kind of blue eyed boy.

Although she was very soft and polite but then she was only making her investigation on Pappi and Pappi using his acting skills managed to bring tears in his eyes and tried to look ashamed of his deed. He thought he looked cute when he did that, to me it looked stupid and silly. She asked him to come with her in the lab and talk.

As Pappi went with her to the lab, everyone in the class started talking '*yaar Aayush ro diya* (guys Aayush is crying) if he speaks up then all of us are screwed.'

In the lab she said, "Aayush you are a good boy, you study well but why do you run with all such guys its not good beta." Pappi continued his innocent looks and said, "Madam I'm not good."

"No who told you this? I'm telling you that you are a good boy." Pappi again said the same thing. But she kept insisting and was trying to make him a good boy and treating him like her son and Pappi was continuously telling her that he was not good.

Then after sometime she asked him, "Fine tell me what I should do? I want to call your parents and arrange a meeting with the Principal."

Pappi kept his innocent looks on and said, “Madam this will not happen again and I will not run from now on.”

“Fine then what about others.”

“How can I guarantee about them ma’am?”

“I have a good impression for you, but the problem is if I leave you I will have to leave the whole class.”

After thinking for sometime and looking at his innocent face she said, “Fine this time I’m leaving you and the whole class but you will have to promise me that you will never run again.” Pappi made the promise and Alka madam spared the whole class.

After this interaction Pappi came back into the class as everyone was looking at him curiously. Pappi declared, “If I run now she will not leave me. This time around she is letting us go.”

After the lecture everybody went to Pappi in sympathy and tried to comfort him. Pappi said, “What guys what happened arey I was not tense, I was just acting.” Hearing this everyone laughed and thanked him for saving and said to him that he was a great actor and a great man too.

On that day all of us decided to run again and we also took Pappi with us. Well most of us thought that he will save their ass once again. Well

Pappi for sure enjoyed this attention and importance in class, becoming the hero for class or rather the saviour for class, he sure enjoyed such things which brought glamour and glory to him.

12

FRIEND, TRAITOR AND A WONDERFUL GIFT

All this while my love for Abhishikta was growing by leaps and bounds and I was waiting for an opportunity or rather I should say help to gather more information about her; her family, her likes and dislikes. Also I was looking for a good coaching for Chemistry. My search ended at the P.K Chemistry classes.

After a couple of weeks of joining the classes I met a guy named Shekar from Campion School. Campion was the most famous boys' School in Bhopal. All the students there were from the rich families. Their parents were bureaucrats, rich businessman and big shot bureaucrats; in short the students were mostly spoilt brats with loads of moolah as their pocket money.

Shekar lived near my home. He was nicknamed Lailu Lapetu by his schoolmates and was famous for his embellish statements. He had an attractive physique which would have attracted quite a few girls towards him and to prove it he also had a few girlfriends.

Our friendship started off well and when I was confident enough I told him about Abhishikta and my love for her. Probably that was the mistake which took away whatever chances I had to get my love Abhishikta. Feels like everything is back to square one where things started almost 11 years ago.

One day Shekar told me about his classmates named Seemant who was the son of some big shot in M.P's bureaucratic scenario. He was allegedly one of the biggest admirers of Abhishikta.

Few days later when I reached the class and was parking my Hero Puch, one of the arrogant guys' with a Nazi type of attitude named Ajeet came with another guy and said, "Is your name Anupam?"

"Yes."

"*Yaar,* have heard a lot about you."

"Really? What is the connection? And by the way who are you?"

The other guy replied, "I am Seemant and the connection is Abhishikta."

"Abhishikta? What about her?"

"Yaar you stop chasing her and stop looking at her." I looked at him in question.

Ajeet said, "Seemant is senti about her and he doesn't want anyone to come in between him and Abhishikta."

"Is Abhishikta his girlfriend?"

"You can say so?"

"Means she isn't; so if she isn't his girlfriend then why doesn't he go and make efforts there instead of trying to bully and pick up a fight with anyone and everyone who likes Abhishikta." This pissed off Seemant.

Ajeet said, "Listen, we are warning you, don't come in between Seemant and Abhishikta, or else we will break your bones."

"Well if you can break my bones I can at least break your nose, by the way I am not in anybody's way or coming in between anyone and still if you think it is that way then the day Abhishikta becomes his girlfriend officially I will not come in between both of them."

The next day when I met Shekar at his home I told him about the previous evening. Shekar said, "Don't worry I will talk to him and things will be fine."

"Yes that would be good, no point getting indulged in unnecessary fights over someone who is neither his nor mine."

That evening Shruti called up. Shruti is my cousin and she is my sweetheart, one the five most beautiful women in my life; ranking my mom at number one. All these years, whatever has happened in my life, she has stood by me. I can still remember the day she gave me the most valuable gift I have ever got in my life, a photograph of Abhishikta. The photograph was clicked by Shruti at the School farewell function of Abhishikta's batch. Abhishikta was wearing a black silk saree with golden yellow border.

When Shruti called up I told her everything that happened in the coaching. She said, "*Bhai* be careful, there will be loads of guys' of influential parents behind her."

"I don't care honey; all I know is that I love her and that's it."

"I know *bhai*, but be careful, I'm always worried about."

"I know that honey."

"*Accha* tell me when are you coming tomorrow for rakhi."

"Oh! I forgot completely, will be there in afternoon honey."

Souls for love and fear.

My love for Abhishikta was growing every day in my heart and my condition was such that there was not a single day when I could think of living without looking at her beautiful face. I was head over heels in love with her. I spoke to her few times when we were with sir clearing our doubts or when we were alone in the class waiting for sir.

Those were the days when it seemed as if there was a breeze of love flowing everywhere and the cupid finding enough soft and easy targets. I dreamt of Abhishikta; Rana for Renuka and Abhishek for Shalini. In all this Pappi was the only one left out. Well it was kind of a surprise that Mr.*Aaashiq* (Mr. Lover) aka Pappi didn't come up with any crushes or infatuation based love till now.

One fine day cupid aimed Pappi with arrow of Rinki and hit Pappi; the love arrow went straight through his heart and made a dent good enough to last a whole lifetime.

That day in the afternoon Pappi was wandering on the terrace, when he saw Rinki coming on the terrace of her home with a chair and book in her hand, she didn't notice Pappi, sat with her book and started reading.

As Rinki was busy reading the book Pappi was busy glancing at her beautiful face. Pappi was so lost in her face that he didn't even notice that Rinki had stopped reading and was now looking at Pappi. Pappi waved at her and Rinki smiled back at him.

That smile made love bloom in Pappi's heart for Rinki.

One day Pappi noticed a boy passing by her house staring at her house for few seconds and then the boy left. This repeated for the next 3-4 days. Pappi became curious; he wanted to know who this boy was and obviously getting insecure by the new competition. He told this to Harshit and Harshit agreed to the observation made by Pappi. One day they were standing at the corner of the road to catch that boy, he came towards the turn and they started walking towards him but he saw them advancing towards him and he ran away.

Pappi's love for Rinki was growing exponentially as a breed of micro-organisms grow in an habitat which is full of nutrition and his SRK qualities kept coming in his expressions for love of Rinki. He played songs of *Kuch Kuch Hota Hai* (a Bollywood movie featuring SRK), whenever Rinki passed by his house and she smiled at him.

One day he said to me, “Yaar I will die if I do not tell her about my feelings. I’m not able to find out whether she loves me or not and this is bugging me even more.”

I said to “Dude talking directly to Rinki might hammer your image in the neighbourhood.”

“Then what do I do?”

“Well we can do Planchette, Rana and I had heard that, most of the predictions are true. Want to try it for Rinki?”

“Is there any risk in doing Planchette?”

“Well dude the risks in these matters are always high. But it’s worth it.”

Pappi agreed to it and said, “But we need a place to do it.”

“Well about the place you arrange for it and Rana is good at drawing. I’m sure he will join in.”

Later that evening Pappi spoke to Abhishek about this and Abhishek saw this as a good opportunity to get some predictions about him and Shalini, so he readily agreed.

So we were at the Abhishek's house for performing the famous Black Magic of Bengal. We started the act by pulling down all the curtains and the room was dark, well that was because no one should even get a slight inkling of what we were upto.

I said, "*Yaar keep* the curtains open at least we will be able to see what the Spirit is telling us, in pitch darkness how will we see. So the curtains were opened enough to use the visual sense.

Pappi asked me about the art of Planchette which supposed to be was some kind of black magic or wizardry for communication with souls. I told him that souls who did not find *Moksha* after they died would respond to these calls and would come and answer questions. For example a person who might have been murdered would not get *Moksha* until his or her killer would be brought to justice. Pappi was thrilled to hear it and he asked more about it I said there are various ways of doing it, some high level practices which required going to a shamshaan bhoomi or a graveyard and then practising spells, now Pappi got a bit frightened and said, "Isn't there an easier way of doing it where the risks of a ghost occupying your body are far lesser."

"Yes I have heard of one such way but never practiced it."

"What's that?"

"In this you need a cap of a bottle like the pet bottle of soft–drinks and a piece of paper where we needed to draw some circles and then place the cap on the circles with each one of the performing member would put their fingers on the cap and then call for the soul of the dead."

“Okay do you know what to draw?”

“Yes and Rana is already on it.”

Abhishek asked me, “But will the answers given by this soul be right or not?”

“I don’t know the answer to that but I have heard that if the spirit is not evil then answers are right.”

Rana completed the chart we placed the bottle cap in the centre and put our index finger tip at it and started calling upon the soul together after sometime the cap started moving I said, “I think the spirit has already arrived.”

Pappi said, “Now what do we do?” I described to him in brief on how to check for the correctness of the spirit.

I asked, “Holy Soul if you have come and entered the cap please move to yes.” The cap moved to yes. Then I requested it to move back to start. Pappi confirmed by the same silly stupid question, “Could you please tell me the colour of my underwear?” I felt like laughing out loud but then controlled. The cap showed the alphabets B.R.O.W.N, all of us looked at Pappi and Pappi said in surprise, “Yes it’s true.”

We let Abhishek quench his thirst of questions first.

Abhishek asked questions related to Shalini.

Now it was Pappi's turn now to ask his questions. But Pappi and his questions were irritating and how can this not irritate a good holy soul, as soon as Pappi started his questions the cap started to move all over the sheet of paper making vicious circles; we got petrified by this and Pappi was the most terrified among us. He said, "What's happening buddy?"

I said, "May be the soul is now getting irritated and doesn't want to answer the questions, may be we should let it go and then call some other soul after sometime." We took a break of 30 minutes then we again started the act this time we called a different soul and after the checks and confirmation Pappi again started with his questions. His first question was related to love, "Does Rinki love me?" this time the answer was a positive one, we saw the cap move to the circle marked yes. The next question came, "When should I propose her?" the cap moved and gave the word 'March'; seeing this Pappi became sad as he wanted to propose ASAP. I asked him to calm down and continue the questions, next question came, "What will be the name of the girl to whom I will be married?" the cap moved to S E E M A, but there was no Seema in his life so we thought, may be later on Pappi would again fall in love with someone named Seema or may be his parents would find him a girl named Seema but this was depressing for Pappi because he wanted to get married to Rinki. He loved her too much and didn't think of anyone else. Pappi continued, "Will I clear PET?" the answer came no; next question was, "Will I be able to pass in 12th standard board exams?" the answer came yes; next question was, "How much percentage I will score in 12th?" the answer came 77; next question was, "How much marks will I get in Maths?" the answer came 91; next question, "Will I be able to become an engineer?" the answer came yes; this was surprising for all of us as we all knew that for doing engineering in M.P one is required to clear the MPPET exam and the soul had already mentioned that Pappi won't be clearing the MPPET exam, but as I have always say 'Let some questions be answered by future' so we left the answer to this question to future and destiny.

Pappi like Abhishek was truly obsessed by love at that point of time, so questions like MPPET and Engineering really didn't matter to him or even if it mattered probably it was on the least priority. After this Rana and I asked few questions and respectfully let the soul go. I said to Pappi, "So dude wassup on your mind?"

Love smitten Pappi replied, "Lets see because most of the questions I asked are hidden somewhere in future so lets wait for the right time." But one thing Pappi wanted to do was to propose Rinki ASAP. I advised Pappi to take sometime and then propose her; but a love smitten Pappi never listens to anyone and then ends up creating hell over love.

One day while having our NAVY Cut near School tapri Pappi said, “Yaar I have quit the idea of loving and proposing Rinki, suppose if she says yes I will also get ghostly attacks, its going to be a buy one get one free kind of offer, marry Rinki and get one ghost absolutely free.”

Somewhere in his mind he was afraid of Rinki as she also had a ghostly experience and our Pappi gets horrified by ghosts as George Bush gets terrorised by Osama Bin Laden.

I said, “Look dude this is not right. You can’t just stop loving her because she was attacked by some ghost ages ago. She was not at fault for that. Fine if you don’t want to love her or propose her, but then don’t blame her for something for which she is not responsible.” But Pappi was so frightened that he refused and denied all our talks.

One night around mid–night Abhishek went to Pappi’s house and asked him to accompany him; Pappi asked, “Where are we going?”

“Don’t ask questions just hop on the bike.”

He took him to a place which was kind of small woods. The place was dark and nobody went there during night. There was a tamarind tree which was supposed to be a hideout for ghosts; also there were a lot of iron nails hammered into the tree. People said that those nails were bound by magical mantras which held ghosts as prisoners. If anyone plucked out any nail the ghost would enter his or her body. Pappi said, "Abhishek drop me back home and then do whatever you wish to do."

"I have brought you here to end your fear of ghosts." Saying this he pulled out an iron nail from the tree; nothing happened to him. After this he started smoking a cigarette and started wetting the tree by his Pee. Pappi said, "Don't do that. No one disrespects this Imli tree." But Abhishek didn't listen and continued to drain his kidney on the tree and nothing happened to him.

After this they came back, but Pappi was so terrified that he couldn't sleep that night.

One day while returning from coaching Pappi asked Abhishek to go to the NCC grounds where Pappi lit a cigarette and said, "Buddy I love Rinki and now no matter what I'm not afraid and will keep on loving her for the rest of my life. I will make sure that she is free from every evil spirit and I will do everything for her."

This was the first time that Pappi had taken a right decision and I felt that this was really true love which made Pappi say these words, whether or not he would get his love, but this feeling of love to sacrifice himself for Rinki was the greatest feeling I had ever seen in Pappi. Most of the times his head is full of silly obsessions and stupid thoughts, but this time I could make out that Pappi was really serious this time for love; love which would make him smile and cry, a love which he would never forget for his entire life time and neither would I.

One day while smoking NAVY Cut in nearby woods to School Abhishek said, “Guys I hear strange noises and objects are missing or misplaced or sometimes they are banged hard on ground in my house, this happens mostly at night.”

To which *fattu* (coward) Pappi said “I think there is a ghost in there.”

Rana said, “It might be due to the plantchette that we were able to call the spirit to ask questions but were not able to send it back properly and it has become powerful.”

I said “You fuking fattus Abhishek only has a doubt we need to have proof as far as I know there is nothing that hurted him or his brother, am I right Abhishek?”

“Yes, but my parents are coming next week and I need to solve this problem as soon as possible.”

“Ok then we will stay at your home for two or three nights to find out if there’s anything.” I said.

Two days later we all were sleeping in the hall, Pappi was sleeping fully covered with blanket as he did not want to have any view of ghost and he did not want any ghost to spot him. Around 2am Rana woke up thirsty and went to kitchen, he was half sleep he tried to open the refrigerator but it opened automatically, he thought it might be some new technology, but suddenly he heard a noise as if someone moved the dining chair in the kitchen, now he was wide awake with horror, his feet felt heavy as if someone had grabbed his feet. He moved out of kitchen. Passing by the master bedroom he saw someone probably a lady or girl staring at dressing table wearing a bra and a panty, he rushed out. He came back to the hall and tried to wake me up but suddenly he heard a voice whispering in his ears.

"Lay down or else I will enter you and will burst your head."

The voice was manly with a female touch to it.

He was scared to death; slowly he felt the blanket covering him and a body sliding over him.

He was in a state of paralysis and some kind of pyshic attack due to which he wasn't able to protest.

He realized his pants being pulled down and removed he wanted to shout but he couldn't, his clothes were removed one by one. He then felt a violation through his body and then slowly his body started to move back and forth, his ass started paining.

I woke up to piss at around 2:30am and saw that Rana was moving to and fro in his blanket I thought he was having another of his intimate sessions with the girl of his dreams, in his dreams and this *"khaat kabaddi"* was a part of it. I moved towards the toilet but then I heard two moaning voices one was Rana's and the other one I could not relate to, I went to have a close look, I saw two pair of legs out of the blanket and switched on the lights. I uncovered the blanket and "whoooo…"

My eyes were wide open, I was looking at the unimagineable, Rana was laid below wide spread and someone was over him, a male body having orgasm. I pushed the other body over Rana and it was another shock, it was Anurag, Abhishek's brother, he had lipstick on his lips and was wearing bra; the panties were lying on the floor. I couldn't understand this gayish fetish; lots of questions were running in my mind. But I had to end this; I slapped Anurag and Rana. The impact of the slaps was so strong that Rana came out of his current state. Everyone was awake, suddenly Anurag screamed in a girl's voice, "I will kill all of you bastards," his scream was loud and scary and it was very much clear that he wasn't acting but it was real.

"You stopped me from fulfilling my desires."

We tried to catch him but he somehow he got extraordinary strength, unusal power; it was something else. We tied his hands and made him sit on a chair, Pappi brought *hanumanji's* (Hindu GOD) photo and started chanting hanuman chalisa hearing it Anurag started crying "Leave me leave me don't burn me" and he fainted.

We were scared and prayed for the sun to rise soon. It was confirmed that there are paranormal activities in Abhishek's house and now Anurag is haunted with a spirit.

I asked Pappi to find out the 'tantrik' who helped Rinki to recover. Pappi found him and after some kriya's done by tantrik, the haunted house of Abhishek returned to normal.

13

ABHISHIKTA

It was on 7th of July 2008 when I sent her a birthday e–greeting hoping that may be now she would realize how much I love her. 3 days later I started writing this book. This book I dedicate to you my love, to tell you everything I did and why I did, which probably you never understood. I don't know whether this tribute would be able to go straight into her heart with love.

Abhishikta, the most beautiful girl for my eyes, the most beautiful face for my senses, the most beautiful feeling of my heart, the most wonderful experience I have ever had in my life.

Abhishikta lived at one of the most posh colonies in Bhopal which was meant for top bureaucrats. A core Cancerian she was an intelligent girl. She was the only girl I had ever seen who would match the specifications of ‘Beauty with Brains’.

Nicknamed ‘Eina’ she was the kind of beauty that guys would kill for. The more number of boys’ knew her the more boys’ fell in love with her.

It was 5th of July 1999, 6 O’clock in the evening. “Hello” was my first word in a very nervous tone and a shaky voice. “Hello” the reply from the sweetest voice in my life. I said, “Hi Happy Birthday.”

“Thanks, but who is it?” ‘How dumb of me, how is she supposed to know that it’s Anupam?’

I said, “Oh! Sorry, it’s Anupam here.”

“Oh! Hi Anupam! How are you? Thanks for calling.”

“I’m fine thanks. Had to call up, it’s your birthday.”

“So many thanks and thanks for calling. But how did you know it’s my birthday today?”

“Not a big thing for someone who likes Abhishkta.”

“Likes?”

“Don’t worry about that, and by the way wish your sister a Happy Birthday as well.”

"Sure."

"What's the plan today?"

"Waiting for my friends to come then would go somewhere for a treat."

"Cool, wish I could get a treat as well."

"Yes sometime sure."

"Thanks and how are the studies going on?" I thought, 'what the fuck, you didn't call up to discuss Mathematics theorems or laws of physics.' I didn't know what to say and was too afraid to say I Love You, so the only thing which came to my instincts was studies.

Abhishikta said, "It's going fine, hope to clear the competitive exams this year." Just then I heard a shout in female voice, "Eina! They are here, let's go."

I asked, "Who's that?"

"My sister, my friends are here so have to go. Speak later."

"Ohkie, enjoy the day and once again Happy Birthday."

"Thank you and thanks for calling, take care, bye." Beep Beep Beep, Click. She hung up. The way she said 'take care' and 'Bye' was the softest tone and accent I had ever heard. Those two words became the flavour of my life. Why did someone have to break the lovely conversation I was having with my love. After paying the bill I moved out, a thought came to me 'she must be out of her house now and if I rush I could get a glance of her.' I was at the calling booth behind her house. I jumped on my Hero Puch and raced towards her house. I made it just in the nick of time to see her getting into a car. The car made a 'U' turn and then came straight towards me, as the car crossed, I saw Abhishikta and she saw me, she passed a smile. Oh! I so loved her, I so loved her, just loved her.

A few days later Shekar told me that Seemant who was in love with her truly, madly, deeply has suddenly started going around with some other girl. The reasons were first his father came to knew about his crush and asked him to stop thinking about her. The second was that one of his friend liked Abhishikta and he asked Seemant to move out of way, so Seemant sacrificed his love for his friend's liking.

Wow! What love? First he doesn't know whether Abhishikta loves him or not, second he even doesn't know that Abhishikta likes his friend or not, but the sacrifice sounded of the highest quality.

I called Abhishikta many times and had good time speaking with her and was sure that by now she knows about my liking for her. At times Shekar would call her under my name and speak to her, no it was not that he committed fraud but I asked him to do that as on those days I didn't feel confident enough to talk to her in my own voice but I really needed to hear her voice badly. All the time when Shekar was on call with her pretending to be me, I used to listen to the conversation over a parallel phone and I just hoped that one day when I would be able to have Abhishikta as my girlfriend and then wife. When I would tell her this she would understand it as my love for her. My dying desire to hear her voice to keep myself alive was not a fraud act.

I did the F.L.A.M.E.S compatibility. F.L.A.M.E.S. was a little game popularly played by teenagers by sratching name of yourself and the person you think you love and figure out what the relation would be, the last remaining letter would denote the relationship you would end up having with the person. The index goes like F = Friends, L = Love, A = Affair, M = Marriage, E = Enemy, S = Sister. Whenever I did it I wished for Marriage but it always came out to be the Alphabet 'L' which meant love. I had mixed feelings on that, as it never came out to be marriage which made me sad but used to jump with joy like a kid who got his favourite chocolate upon seeing 'L' which meant love. I wished that may Abhishikta too plays F.L.A.M.E.S. with my name and sees this. But I never knew that I would never be able to get

Abhishikta as my wife, even after loving her for 10 years she would not understand my feelings and hate me to her heart's content.

Came October'99 and it was Diwali, for me it was an opportunity to call Abhishikta and hear the sweetest voice on this planet.

I dialled her number and to my luck she picked up the phone. Maybe she knew that I would call up or maybe she was expecting someone else's call, I don't know. I said, "Hello." The sweetest voice replied, "Hello"; I said, "May I speak to Miss Abhishikta please." The sweetest voice said, "Yes, Abhishikta here, who is this?"

"Hi, Anupam here."

"Hi Anupam, how are you?" that enthusiasm in her voice made me feel like I'm on heaven. I just died in her love once again. I wanted to cling to that receiver forever and wished she kept saying 'Hi' to me with that tone and accent forever.

She said, "Hello! Are you there?"

I said, "How are you?"

"I'm fine."

"Wish you a very happy diwali."

"Thank you so much and wish you a very happy diwali too."

"Thanks, so wassup for the celebrations?"

"Just finished with the puja, and your call came so I'm now talking to you"

I felt so lucky.

I said, "So what's the plan after we hang up or you wish me to keep talking for the whole night, which by the way is highly advisable and I would prefer celebrate my Diwali that way."

She laughed, "Well there are plans; waiting for my friends to come then would fire some crackers that's it."

"So not going out?"

"No, it's too dangerous to go out on Diwali night and then guests keep coming so have to be at home for them."

"Yes with all that make up and heavy dresses it's really tough to go out."

"Yeah. And wassup with you? Celebrating?"

"Naa not really, at home, let's see if some friend comes along then could go out. Anyways I can't celebrate without seeing you."

"What?"

"Well I mean you are my good friend so without good friends it's tough to do any kind of celebration."

"Oh! Yes I know it's boring to have any festival without friends."

"Yes but at least we have got telephone and now that I have heard your voice I can celebrate Diwali." She laughed at that. I just loved that, it was all so romantic for me. Then as usual my luck ran out of fuel as I heard, "Eina! Happy Diwali!" The unheard statement was, 'Anupam! Sad Diwali!'

Eina said, "Hi. Happy Diwali; just give me a second I'm on phone with someone." Then she said to me, "Anupam I have to go, my friends are here."

"Yeah sure my time ends now."

"Nothing like that, we will speak soon."

"Just joking, enjoy with you friends; see you soon, bye."

"Thanks for calling, take care, bye." Just then I heard 'Anupam!' someone yelling my name at the top of his voice. I went out and saw Byju; we wished each other Diwali by hugging. Byju said, "Chal."

"Where?"

"Will go and meet some friends." As we started I said, "Yaar take me to New market."

"Why?" I told him about my talks with Abhishikta and I told him that I wanted to see Abhishikta on this day. Byju said, "Okay dude, New market it is." At New market as we crossed Abhishikta's house I saw Abhishikta with her friends firing some crackers as I passed she gave me a smile and waved at me like saying 'Hi'; that was a great moment for me. She was looking absolutely stunning, breathtakingly beautiful. Byju almost stopped his scooter there and I just kept gazing at her beautiful face.

My eyes or my mind didn't read or recognize anything else, no other face was readable by my memory, my eyes fixed at that distance where her face was and the adjustable properties of my retina failed to respond. I recalled the 'take care' which she had said almost half an hour ago and I just fell more deep in her love. I just wanted to go near her and say, '*You have the most beautiful hair, could you keep them open like this for me for the rest of my life. You have the most beautiful lips, can I keep kissing them rest of my life. You have the most beautiful voice, can I keep hearing you for the rest of my life, you are the angel of my life, will you always be my angel of life.'* I smiled at her and she flashed that billion dollar sorry trillion dollar, no that invaluable smile at me. That look of her's was the attack which caused my heart skip a beat and even today after 10 long years whenever I close my eyes and recall that smile my heart skips a beat.

After that I came back home. 5 minutes later I heard the shout 'Anupam!' once again. This time it was Shekar. I told him everything that happened that evening and once again I set off towards New market with Shekar. That day I would have got anything I wished, as I wished that I would be able to see her again and Yo! There she was standing right there at the gate of her home and chatting with her friend. She saw me, smiled and gave her neck a slight swaying movement as if saying, 'Fine I know you are in love with me and you have spoken to me and seen me as well, now go and celebrate Diwali with your friends.' This time I noticed she had worn a deep blue coloured saree looking astonishing, stunning, breathtaking and smashing. As usual she had that paralysing effect on me; my heart stopped beating and started chanting 'Abhishikta', 'Abhishikta', 'Abhishikta'. That evening I was trying hard not to make an eye contact with those lovely eyes to avoid going into coma and stay alive; today after 10 years I'm trying hard to make at least one eye contact with those lovely deep eyes and stay alive.

After that evening we met several times in coaching and I spoke to her. Whenever she spoke to some guy although my heart was on fire but there was one thing which I noticed and really liked, admired and adored about her. It was her maturity. Abhishikta's maturity was proven by the fact that she behaved like a well mannered lady at all times.

Such is the beauty of my love 'Abhishikta'. But destiny had some other plans about this lady in my life. For me she was to be set up like an untouched goddess in a temple and untouchables like me could only worship her from a distance. I could only dream about having her in my home – as my wife.

Sometimes I think I was fool to fall so quickly in love with her, and even bigger fool to keep that love for Abhishikta alive even today, after 10 yrs of falling in love with her. But that probably is the only foolish thing that I relish even today. Destiny and despicable friends took her away from me. Today after 10 long years of being in love with her, my love and my life still remains UNTITLED.

14

NAVY CUT IS A NATIONAL ASSEST, SAVE IT

Our School bunking sessions continued with that our fun and parties too. By this time our frequency of visits to Bhojpur had also increased. Well to be honest they were picnics to Bhojpur. Bhojpur is a small place, almost 28 kilometres from Bhopal situated on the banks of river *Betwa*. Bhojpur is famous for India's largest shiva lingam in a temple which is called *Bhojeshwar*. It is a famous destination among all Lord Shiva devotees and every year during Mahashivratri the flood of devotees just keeps increasing exponentially. But our trips were scheduled as short picnics and that too mainly times when there were no important Lord Shiva's celebrations; we also avoided going there on Monday's because of heavy rush of devotees.

That day was a Wednesday. The beginning of December when Rana, Pappi, Abhishek and I escaped from School. I had my Hero Puch and Abhishek had his TVS scooty we already had the plans to go to Bhojpur. Well making a plan for a Bhojpur trip was not a new thing, but this time the added feature of Alcohol was a new thing and an exciting as well. That day we came fully prepared with bedsheets tucked into our bags and a set of clothes, towels and fresh underwear. The idea was to have a full fledged picnic at Bhojpur by the river *Betwa* and have a swim in *Betwa* as well. After we escaped out it was decided that Pappi would be my pillion on Hero Puch and Rana would be Abhishek's pillion on his scooty. The two members of each vehicle would have to share the petrol expenses among themselves rest all other expenses would be divided by four to find out per head cost. We picked our bikes and raced towards Bhojpur. We reached Habibganj Naka from where the highway number 12 started which led to Bhojpur. The Habibganj Naka is a hub of activities, shops and tapris of everything can be found there. Our main concern was Alcohol. Pappi and I wanted to have beer and Rana and Abhishek wanted to have whiskey. There was debate on what to buy. I said, "Let's buy *daaru* (Alcohol) once we are outside the city limits. We will get it at a less price there and we can discuss what to buy, here if we are seen by some uncle infront of a wine shop discussing things then we all are doomed." They all agreed and we started off upon crossing the city limits we came to a place called *Misrod.* It was a small place on the highway. We saw a wine shop and we halted for purchasing our quota of liquor for the picnic. The discussion again became hot and Rana said, "Yaar I won't drink beer, it smells like sewage water."

Abhishek said, "Horse piss."

I said, "But we want to have beer only, it is *somras* dude." After a lot of heated discussion we settled on three bottles of Kingfisher beer and a half bottle of Mc Dowells No. 1 whiskey. Those were the golden days for people who drank and smoke when liquor and cigarettes were affordable. The whole lot of liquor cost us somewhere close to 235 Rupees which came to a mere 58.75 Rupees per head. We also got two packets of NAVY Cut cigarettes, four plastic cups, a bottle of coca–cola, couple of packs of salted peanuts and a couple of packs of salted potato chips and continued our journey towards Bhojpur. At the road junction of Mandideep and Bhojpur we stopped as Abhishek had to refuel his scooty, Pappi said, "Yaar even you check if we need refuelling."

I said, "Don't worry dude, my Hero Puch has got enough petrol to go back to Bhopal from Bhojpur and then again come back to Bhojpur and anyways my bike is Hero Puch dude, it's the most fuel efficient vehicle in its category."

"Great then we can have a puff at the *tapri* while Abhishek refuels his scooty." After Abhishek refilled his scooty and we finished our puff our journey towards Bhojpur continued, it took us around 20 minutes more to reach Bhojpur as the roads depicted the typical Indian roads with a swimming pool in the middle of the road at a chainage of every 100 mts. Upon reaching Bhojpur everyone wanted to go to the temple for a small prayer to Lord Shiva. I said, "Dudes you are here to have whiskey and beer party and before that you want to go to the temple? What the *fuck yaar*?"

Pappi said, "*Yaar* Alcohol is the favourite drink of Bhole Baba. So don't worry."

"Fine but then the pandits of the temple won't allow us with Alcohol bottles in our bags and enter the temple premises."

"True, these pandits they themselves drink inside the temple premises but they won't allow us."

"Okay you three go to the temple I will wait outside once you guys come back we will head towards the river."

"What aren't you coming to pay a visit to Lord Shiva?"

"No." My answer was firm and kind of determined so no one said anything about it. All three of them went inside the temple and I guarded the bags and their shoes outside the temple. After almost 15 minutes they came back and we headed towards the river *Betwa*.

The river *Betwa* in Bhojpur near the *Bhojeswar* temple flows through large rocks which were supposed to be part of a huge Cyclopean dam constructed by the Parmar King Raja Bhoj. The huge rocks along the banks of the river restrict the river current to a minimum and in winter season when the flow of the river is perfect and the sunshine is also perfect in the chill of Bhopal it is the right time to have a bath in the river and have a grand riverside picnic on the rocks alongside the banks. One has to climb downhill to reach the river banks and the picture perfect location for picnic. Once we reached the banks we kept strolling along the banks of the river until we found a location which was perfect for us. The place we chose was a location where the width of the river was reduced to a bare 8–10 feet because of huge rocks and further downstream the width got even more narrow may be a couple of meters and the depth was not much. The choice of this location was made keeping in consideration that since none of us were swimmers if we happen to slip while in the waters we have a chance of holding on to the big rocks and the narrow passage would give a chance of locking our bodies in the passage and save us. Also the large rocks on the either sides gave a flat surface and received ample sunshine to beat the chill of the ceinate and the water. After deciding on the picnic spot we spread out the bed sheets and brought out the beer bottles and the whiskey bottle. Rana made for himself and Abhishek; Pappi and I took one beer bottle each and with large cheers we started our picnic, well daaru picnic. After a few gulps of beer the sentiments started flowing out.

I said, “Yaar Pups I really love her.”

“Even I love her yaar.”

“Oye why do you love her?”

“Yaar just like you love her, I too love her.”

“Ok yaar if you love her then I will not come in between both of you.”

“But you were never in between me and Rinki.”

“Oh! Rinki, I thought you were talking about Abhishikta.”

“bhenchod tereko chad gayi hai” (fucker, you are high)

I grinned. Then I saw Abhishek and Rana getting ready to take their plunge into the Betwa waters.

I said, "Dude take care while you take your plunge."

Rana said, "Why don't you guys join in too?" I looked at Pappi and he agreed. Soon we were in the waters of Betwa. The water was chilling but refreshing and under the effect of Alcohol it was even better.

Pappi said, "Yaar I will go and have another gulp of beer."

"Sure dude and get me my bottle." Pappi went and had another big gulp of the Kingfisher and sat down. He took out a piece of paper from the pocket of his trouser and started glaring at it. When I saw Pappi reading through that piece of paper I went and sat besides him and said, "Dude what's that?" Pappi started hiding that piece of paper. I said, "Abey show me what is that? You got another love letter from a girl."

"No yaar." The effect of Alcohol is amazing, it brings out the emotions of heart to your face and on your lips and Pappi was no different. I said, "So you have written a love letter to Rinki."

Pappi shyly said, "Yes."

"Haye haye, see the blush on the face of our SRK. Now show me the letter." Pappi gave me the letter. It was long fangled romantic and sentimental love letter and it was signed Ash at below. I said, "Abey since when did you become Ash from Aayush." Pappi grinned.

I said, "When are you going to give this letter to her?"

"Very soon" Very little did I know that Pappi's 'very soon' would become a pain in our asses real soon. I said, "Dude just keep in mind what the Spirit said and take any step forward only when the time is right."

"Yaar what do I do? I can't live without her. I will die if I don't get her." Sensing that the situation of fun and frolic was getting heavy by the sentiments and that too under the action of an alcoholic beverage I said, "Chal yaar, lets enjoy the picnic now will think later on what to do. Lets have a puff and get back into the water." We lighted a NAVY Cut had a few puffs and then Pappi said, "Yaar lets get into the water and we can keep smoking in the cool waters." I nodded and I went back into the river. Pappi followed me but by this time his intoxication level was quite high and with all the partying he was already a mix bag of emotions in his mind. He entered the waters and wanted to keep his best foot forward for a firm grip at the base, but as usual his best foot ditched him under the effect of Alcohol and CHAPAK! He was drowning; I jumped; not to save him but to save the NAVY Cut in his hand but alas! By the moment I reached the cigarette it was all wet when I stood up with the wet cigarette in hand I saw Pappi stuck up in a rock struggling to get out of the watery mess. I gave him my hand, he stood up and said, "*bhanchod*, I was drowning and you jumped for that bloody cigarette. Is this is what your friendship, let the friend die and save cigarette?"

"Idiot first you wasted one full cigarette and then you call NAVY Cut 'bloody cigarette', do you know this is a national asset we pay taxes on this which goes for the development of nation. Wasting it is serious crime, and even after saving you, you are blaming me. Shame on you."

"So what you are my best friend and instead of saving my life first you jumped after the cigarette."

"Wrong, I didn't jump after the cigarette I jumped after a national asset which was put to risk by a sinner like you, but alas even my dying efforts couldn't save the national asset. See national assets are gone so easily but sinners like you don't go down so easily."

I asked him. "Tell me if I were drowning with a cigarette in my hand, which would you have saved first."

To this Pappi said, *"Pran jaye toh jaye par cigarette naa jaye"* (Between life and cigarette, always choose cigarette).

By the time we finished our drinks it was almost 3.00 P.M. in afternoon and we had to go back.

Rana said, "Hey why don't we try a different route." I knew he was knocked out by the whiskey but this was something insane.

Pappi said, "What different?"

Rana said, "Let's not go back by the way we came down. Let's try the trekking way."

I said, "The Alcohol has fucked your whole brain. Are you nuts?"

Abhishek said, "No yaar, Rana is right we should try something tougher."

I said, "If you are interested in doing something tough then take up the IIT / JEE exams and that too in full senses of yours and then you can have some real challenge."

Rana said, "Whatever but I'm going that way." And he started off with Abhishek on his trail. I looked at Pappi and Pappi said, "*Bhai*, we need to go after them who knows what the hell will they land into." So we joined them at the start of the trek Pappi led the way followed by Abhishek, Rana and then me.

Pappi took the first step and this time his best foot was firm enough and did not let him down and he climbed up Abhishek followed him and Rana too took his first step on the rock, his best foot slipped and THUD! He fell; not just he fell, he fell upon me.

I said, "You fucking idiot! I told you that you are not in a condition to walk and you want to trek."

Rana said, "*Aye*, sorry *yaar*, actually I was in some other thoughts."

"You fucker! After gulping so much of daaru who can keep his thoughts on one thing and especially if it's an asshole like you, it's not at all possible."

"*Arre bhai sorry*, now see I will climb the rock with complete balance."

"Huh." For the next 20 minutes Rana kept climbing the rocks and with me behind him, he was on a constant conscious effort that his legs don't waver, but I could see that his legs were shaky and the Alcohol was doing its trick on him; it took a lot of effort on his part to reach the top. Once on top he said, "See I have made it."

I said, "Yes you did, but how, that only I saw. You fool; you could have fallen down on numerous instances and broken your ass on these rocks." He grinned. After grasping O_2 molecules for some time we started towards our bikes, on the way back Rana saw some monkeys and these monkeys became his biggest enemies, well of course under the action of Alcohol. He started throwing stones at them, Pappi seeing this held his hand and pulled him and said, "*Abey* idiot, you shouldn't be drinking daaru. If those monkeys go crazy and attack us they will bloody tear our asses apart in no time." We pulled him back and then took him to our bikes. That evening after I reached home I was in no condition to go to the coaching classes, but I didn't want to miss it, without seeing Abhishikta I would have definitely died. I didn't know at that time that my life would be more miserable than dead in later years when I won't be able to see her at all. If I could re-distribute the limited total quota of seeing Abhishikta in this life then I would have uniformly distributed it over the whole span of my life rather than seeing her daily. That way I would have been alive today.

That evening when I reached the class I was once again seated next to Abhishikta and this time she was looking more beautiful, but my situation was totally down on health terms. The only emotion which held me that evening was Abhishikta. Later that night I was so tired that once I hit the bed I fell asleep at once. But not even in my dreams I had thought that starting next day our lives would be hell and Pappi's would start becoming UNTITLED.

15

THE NUKE OF LOVE

KILLS2

Pappi's freaked out love bug wanted Rinki. Pappi would have proposed the very first day he discovered love, but he refrained because of the fear of Monu, Rinki's brother. Pappi's impression on Monu's was good, if put it in Pappi's words or rather word he would say 'Monu thinks of me as an all-rounder good in studies, sports.' But the negative side was Monu's over protective behaviour towards Rinki; well he was told that Monu had even beaten up a few guys before who had expressed love for Rinki; Beaten Up! Cool! Nice brother huh!

Inspired by one of all time flops of Bollywood '*Pyar kiya to darna kya*' and some atka jhatka crap song of it, he decided to ignore the fear of Monu.

The only good thing was that Pappi was genuinely in love with Rinki and it really showed in his eyes, whenever he spoke about his love philosophy, it sounded silly, but true. Every time Pappi spoke to me about his love life, he was so desperate to propose Rinki and I asked him to have patience and not hurry.

One day after we bunked School we were chilling at Abhishek's place and after some time I saw Pappi was already in his dreams with his dream girl Rinki, I shook him up and said, "*Abey* what are you dreaming?"

"Yaar I can't anymore stand this, I just want to tell Rinki, how much I love her."

"Oye don't get too excited, you should take things easy. If anything goes wrong at this point of time then it might be hard to get them correct at a later time."

"I don't know and I don't care, I just know that I love her and I can't stay even a minute away from her."

I said, "Lets' take some time and confirm at what stage is her feelings for you?" Pappi looked at me amazingly, "But how?"

Abhishek said, “Dude why don’t you call her and tell her your heartfelt feelings.”

Abhishek wanted Pappi to propose Rinki and wanted to see the reaction as for both of them the case was nearly the same and they saw lots of similarities between Rinki and Shalini; well precisely stupid similarities, such as the dress code of both the schools were the same, both of them were commerce students etc. Abhishek thought that if Aayush proposes Rinki and she says ‘Yes’ then his destiny will also be a ‘Yes’ and he will be able to get Shalini and yes one more thing that I forgot to mention, Pappi promised Abhishek that if Rinki says yes to him then Pappi will request Rinki to talk to Shalini about Abhishek. Now this is what I call a bi-lateral deal between two underdeveloped countries for resources.

Pappi dialled her number, the phone rang but luck wasn’t on Pappi’s side and Rinki’s father picked up the phone. Hearing his voice Pappi was frightened and he began to talk in girl's voice to him and said, “Uncleji is Rinki at home, I’m her friend calling.”

“What’s your name?” By now Pappi was so scared stiff, he immediately hung up. We rolled on the floor laughing, he looked so embarrassed and afraid, after several seconds of laughing out loud I said, “Don’t worry dude, it happens, may be you should try sometime later.”

Pappi again dialled the number after a killing gap of 30 minutes and luckily this time Rinki picked up the phone.

She said "Hello"; her voice was like the wind chimes filling in their sweet music in the ears of Pappi which anaesthetized him. He couldn’t utter a word from his mouth, he just stood there, and he was bound by a magical spell, after several seconds when he woke from the magical charm casted by Rinki’s melodious voice. Rinki had already said Hello! ‘N’ number of times and now was getting frustrated; Pappi got afraid of the changing tone of her voice and hung up.

I said, “What happened dude? What did she say?”

“Hello! And I hung up. I don’t know what happened to me, I couldn’t say a word. The moment I heard her voice I went numb.”

“You dumb! You got such a good chance to speak to her and you bloody wasted it.” I shouted at him. Pappi gave me a disappointed look at which I felt bad for him and it was definitely not his fault, even I was spellbound whenever I heard the voice of Abhishikta. It was just that Pappi couldn’t take the joy of hearing the sweetest voice of his life.

I said, “Okay dude, do you want me to write some lines for you, you read it.” Pappi nodded. I quickly wrote the fastest love letter of my life, I guess if there was any media to cover it, it surely would have gone into some kind of record book. Pappi once again dialled the number, again Rinki picked up the phone and said “Hello”.

Pappi said “Hello Rinki.”

“Yes Rinki here. Who's this?”

“Rinki, Pappi here, I want to tell you something, please listen to me and don’t hang up.”

“Pappi? Who Pappi?”

Pappi said, “Pappi!! *pehchaana nahi* (Did you not recognize me)?”

“No.” this made Pappi even more nervous.

“Aayush.”

“Oh! Aayush, yes Aayush, sorry I couldn’t recognize you.”

“It’s okay. I want to tell you something.”

“Yes?” By now the mesmerizing voice of Rinki, the tense atmosphere and no previous experience of proposing a girl had already knocked down Pappi.

He said, “I will tell you but not now.”

"Why not now, that's why you called me. What is it that you want to say? Tell me now, tell me naa."

"No, I don't feel right to say it now. Let the right moment come, then you'll know and everyone else would know as well." Click! Pappi disconnected the line.

Pappi's face had that look of disappointment for missing out but his eyes had a strange spark of love and satisfaction. Well frankly it didn't really matter whether or not Pappi was successful in conveying his words to Rinki, but he was clearly able to pass on his dreams of love to Rinki.

Pappi said, "*Bhai* I was so tensed that I couldn't say a word and it was so of panicky for me yaar."

I said, "Fine dude, no problem, chill you spoke to her and I'm sure after recognizing you she must have definitely got your intentions and that's important at this stage. Let her have some time to digest that and we can think of more appropriate time and way of you proposing to her."

Pappi for the time being took that advice. But the question here was for how long?

Pappi waited for the right moment to come, everyday when he returned from coaching in the morning he followed Rinki till the bus stop from where she would board her School bus, this became a daily Rinkial for him like the bunking of School and doing his daily puja. But with all the efforts Pappi could never get the right moment as the vamp Bindu or Bindu's brother always accompanied Rinki. Pappi found out the leaving hours of the School which was in the afternoon at around 1.00 P.M and expressed to me his wish of chasing her School bus.

Every time Rinki saw Pappi from the window of her School bus Pappi used to sing the song from the movie '*Aradhana*' "*mere sapna ki rani kab aayegi tu, aayi rut (Rinki) mastani kab ayegi tu,*" well to be exact the scene was similar, in the movie the hero and his friend were on a Willys jeep and the heroine on a toy train the Darjeeling types. In our case the jeep was replaced by my Hero Puch and the toy train got substituted by a huge blue coloured TATA bus which emitted such amounts of CO_2, CO and unburnt carbon to kill a person with ease. But those ghastly amounts of killer gases didn't matter to Pappi as he was already dead in love with Rinki.

Love for Rinki was something which made a lot of changes in Pappi, not just the stupid and silly humble things, but he started giving more importance to his appearance, his attire, he always chose carefully what he wore when Rinki was around. It even happened that once Pappi was waiting for Rinki to come out of her home for

School just then his Dad came out saw him and said, "All dressed up, waiting for someone." Pappi was surprised by the sudden arrival of his Dad and said, "What Dad I'm absolutely not waiting for anyone. Now can you please go inside and let me take sun-bath." 'Sun-Bath' huh! That too all dressed up and in the porch. Well his Dad definitely got it, that his son is in love with someone.

It was a sunny day in December at Bhojpur that Pappi after downing a few gulps of Kingfisher super strong beer spoke about Rinki and his plans to propose her. Pappi was serious about it as the Christmas vacations would soon start and then School would close. Pappi's Dad who took his remaining leaves of the year at that time so he won't be able to propose Rinki. Well Pappi had a point and he also wrote his love letter to Rinki. The letter was written in Hindi but when translated to the language of this book, it went something like this:

"Dearest Rinki,

I wanted to tell you something but may be I am not strong enough to say it on your face. Your beautiful face puts up a lock on my lips and your beautiful eyes stop the thought process of my mind. I have never ever realized that all these things make me fall in love with you, the more these things happen; the more I keep falling for you.

For the first time I have started feeling that I have no control over my senses when you are around. I just keep thinking about you all the time, I just can't get you out of my mind and now out of my heart.

My actions have become weird and strange for all my friends, whenever I talk to them; they ask me 'what has happened to you?'

I am unable to understand what this is and I don't want to know what this is, because whatever it is, it's just wonderful. My friends have started saying that I'm in love with you. If this wonderful feeling is love, then yes I'm in love with you and I Love You. I just love you, if ever I have felt such a strange yet wonderful, powerful yet pure feeling within me for anyone, it is just you, yes I Love You Rinki.

I don't know whether you also feel the same for me or not, I don't know whether you like me or not and I don't know whether you love me too or not but I am in deep deep love with you. I just wanted to say this to you and yes if you do not love me and if you are in love with someone else please tell me and I promise that I will never ever cross your road again in my life. But please do tell me what you feel and if you see some abatement in me or my behaviour please do tell me about it I will try to remove it and try to be a guy eligible for your love.

I Love you,

Loving you is all I do all the time,

ASH"

The signing off of the letter was quite awesome Aayush got converted to Ash.

It took him 2 weeks to write this letter, reading and re-writing it all over was all he did for 2 weeks and on that day at Bhojpur after I and Abhishek kind of Okayed it, he decided to present that letter to Rinki.

The next day was the fateful day when Pappi triggered off the nuke of love. He was very positive and was sure that Rinki loved him and she will say yes to him and with the blessing of his Almighty God nothing bad will happen.

Pappi just came from coaching, changed into his best clothes and came out to see whether Rinki is going to School or not but she didn't come out. Disappointed Pappi was about to go back to inside his house, when suddenly he saw the love of his life coming out of her home and luckily today neither the vamp Bindu nor her brother accompanied her. Yes! She was walking alone.

Pappi came out and went behind her. With an envelope which contained a card and the letter in his hand and red rose in other he walked briskly to catch up with her. With a muffler wrapped around his neck he surely was looking like Dev Anand the legendary hero of Bollywood. Rinki was walking with books in her hand and was going through them so she was walking a bit slow that day. Pappi was soon able to catch her up and said, “Hi Rinki.”

Rinki raised one of her eyebrows, “Yes tell me.”

“I called you also over phone but wasn’t able to tell you.”

“Ohh so you were the one who called me.”

“Quickly tell me what you have got to say.” Pappi as usual under the magical effect of presence of Rinki was not able to say anything became completely dumb, but this time he managed to activate his senses and gave her the letter, card and rose and said, “Whatever I wish to say I have written in this letter, please read it whenever you find time.”

“No, I will not take all these please keep it with yourself I don’t want to have this.”

“But why?”

“Just like that I don’t want to take any of these and now you please go otherwise someone will see and it will unnecessarily create trouble for me.”

Pappi stood there, stunned in silence and watched her go and Rinki again looked back and smiled at him.

Although Pappi was disappointed but the last smile from Rinki gave him a new hope that may be she does love him. He was in confusion. Later in the day at School he narrated the entire incident to us. I was a bit disappointed but then the last smile thing was surely morale boosting, as why would a girl reject a love letter and even then smile at the boy. Abhishek said, “Arre sure that she loves you.”

Pappi said, “But why didn’t she take the letter from me?”

“Might be that she wants to hear from you and also there is a chance of someone noticing the love letter and the card.” This made sense and I too agreed to this thought. The remainder of the whole day was too tough for him as he spent the day impatiently for the sun to set and rise again.

The next morning again Pappi put on the best attire, the muffler and went out to see whether Rinki was going to School or not, the moment Rinki came out Pappi started she was reading a book and walking slowly, ‘Oh why does this girl keep reading that damn book everyday, can’t she read my thoughts, my heart’ thought Pappi as he went close to her.

“Hi” said Pappi

"You again! What's wrong with you?"

"I don't know Rinki but I want to tell you something."

This time she smiled and asked, "*Kya* tell me?"

"I Love You," BANG! The nuke of love was exploded. She was shocked to hear explosion of love from almost point blank range and as she saw one of the uncles from neighbourhood passing by she said, "Please Aayush go!"

"No I'll not go until you say yes."

"Aayush please I request you to go now; we can talk some other time, I have my exam today and please let me study." So that was the reason she dug herself deep in the book.

"Ok if you've exam then I'll leave but I Love You and all the best for your exams I know you'll do well."

"Thanks and now please leave and please don't chase me"

"No Rinki I can't do that, I'm in love with you and I'll come every time, till I don't get the answer."

"No Aayush, Please don't do this."

"Ok if your answer is yes then I'll wait outside my house when you return and if you smile then it will be yes or else no." and Pappi left and Rinki moved on towards the bus stand.

After coming back home Pappi was on cloud number nine, he couldn't believe that he had proposed the girl he loved so dearly, he was dancing with joy, it didn't matter for that moment whether Rinki answered or not, it was kind of joy of triumph for him and why not, it's a moment for all boys who successfully manage to propose the girl they have loved the most in their life, the result is immaterial at that point of time. Pappi was confident that it'll be a yes from her side.

That afternoon when he returned from School he saw his brother and sister Pinki, standing out at the main gate waiting for him. His instinct told him that there was a huge after effect from the nuke which he exploded in the morning. Pinki said, "*Bhaiya* you leave from here now, Sehgal Aunty is here and is in a real bad mood after what you did today morning and your mom is also really pissed off about it." Pappi ran off from there and went straight to Abhishek's house and called me and quickly he told me everything that happened he said, "She complained yaar."

"Chill dude, let me come over then we'll see what needs to be done." I rushed off to Abhishek's home where Pappi was already there, sweating in fear. It was already 3pm and our fathers use to return from BHEL factory at around 4pm so I told him to go home and face your mom and Aunty and since your father won't be there, we've a chance of getting things under control.

Pappi said, "Buddy I'm afraid and tense now, will I be able to face them. I never knew that this incident will create too much problems for me; but I was in love and did what everyone does when in love, what else should've I done."

I thought for a while and said, "You have done nothing wrong, but lets face the scene first and then we'll think that why did she complain." Pappi nodded.

I said, "You told me once that there's a guy who moves around Rinki's house pretty frequently."

"Yes. But he doesn't come anymore."

"Cool then go home and let your mom rebuke you a lot and after a lot of interrogation by your mom tell her that, you were being threatened by that guy to do this."

"If she asks for the letter then?"

"Tell her that you tore that away." Pappi looked at me with a question in his eyes.

I said, "Dude we don't have any other option left at this point. And if you want I'll come with you to your home." But Pappi refused and went home alone.

As Pappi entered his home with shaky legs he saw Sehgal Aunty and said, "Namaste Aunty." His mom was furious but all her anger went into the drain the moment she saw her son's innocent face and she calmed down and asked him to sit.

His mom said, "*Beta*, Aunty wants to ask you something."

"*Ji auntyji*"

Sehgal Aunty said, "Beta, what did you say to Rinki today morning."

"I said, I Love You."

"Why *beta*?"

"Actually *auntyji* there's a guy named Anurag. I never met him. One day he caught me and threatened me by saying that he'll beat me if I don't say I Love You to Rinki on his behalf."

"Okay *beta*, even I thought that there was something wrong as you're a very good boy and you don't even talk to Rinki much, so how could you do this? I know this guy Anurag, he used to call Rinki and we've seen him many times in our neighbourhood. We even tried to catch him once but then he ran away, and we've never seen him again. No problem beta but don't do it again and beta don't be afraid of him. If Monu would have come to know about this he would have created a hell out of it he's too touchy you know naa." 'Touchy or Psycho' thought Pappi.

Pappi's mom said, "See I told you naa *Bhabhiji* that my Pappi won't do such a thing, he's a very simple and sober boy."

"*Ji Bhabhiji*, I know that, but please you don't tell about this to Rinki's Papa and Monu, they'll create an unnecessary scene out of it."

"*Bilkul Bhabhiji* and you too don't tell to Pappi's Dad, he'll also create a scene then."

Before Sehgal Aunty left Pappi said sorry to her and asked her to say sorry to Rinki also on his behalf.

Well Pappi saved his ass for the time being but it was only a temporary solution. His mom knew that Pappi has something to do with this, as he was not a guy who would get threatened by anyone so easily and the recent developments in Pappi's behaviour made the doubt go deeper in his mom's mind.

Later in the evening after his Dad came home; over evening tea, Pappi's mom looked at him and said to his father, "*Suniye*, I need to tell you something." Pappi's face grew gloomy with tension and worry. His father asked, "What?"

"First you promise that you won't get angry."

"Ok, but what is it? And what has he done this time?" His mom narrated the whole incident to his father, although his father was a bit angry but he didn't say anything. At dinner time Pappi's father said to him, "*Beta* why did you do like this? You could have told us or you could have ran away with Rinki, we would've handled everything here." Hearing this everyone burst into laughter and Pappi was relaxed and thought 'My Dad is the best Dad in the world'.

The next few days were not going to be good for Pappi for his foolishness. Monu had returned from Delhi and Sehgal Uncle also came back from Sagar but till now they didn't know about the incident or anything related to it.

But as every human being is bound to make mistakes and if that human is Pappi then it's a synonym for mistake.

No one knows what clicked his mind although the theory was to improve his image in the eyes of Rinki and her family, Pappi devised a plan.

One morning while coming back from coaching with Abhishek he said, "I'll tell mom today that the same guy Anurag met me today and threatened to beat me and my brothers. I will ask her to go to Rinki's home and tell them this and if she does it then Rinki and her family will believe me that whatever I said to them was the truth and my impression will again be good in Rinki's eyes." Abhishek was not sure of this, but still he said, "Ok." Upon reaching home Pappi did exactly what he planned and Abhishek became his proof. Pappi's mom got worried and started crying and went straight to Rinki's house and said to her mother, "Bhabhiji, that guy Anurag is again threatening my son and if something happens to him what'll I do." she burst into tears. At that time Sehgal Uncle and Monu were there.

Sehgal Aunty along with uncle came to Pappi's home and as Monu was shaving at that time so Aunty asked him not to come. The reason behind was that Monu was very short-tempered. They all came to Pappi's home, where Pappi was sitting with Abhishek. Pappi told them the fictitious story he had cooked up with Abhishek and Rinki's mom and his mom seemed to agree to that. But Sehgal Uncle though were not convinced he said, "It can't be the way Pappi is saying. Who's that guy? We'll see what he does."

Then Rinki's parents left. Pappi's father was not there at that time, so when he came back, Pappi's mom told him everything.

That evening Sehgal Uncle came to his house along with Sharma uncle who was one of

Pappi's Dad's closest friends in the city and in their neighbourhood as well. Sehgal Uncle used to treat him like his elder brother. Pappi was called and asked a few questions, which Pappi answered and the answers to which annoyed Sehgal Uncle even more.

When I reached his home I saw him standing at the door like a culprit in a courtroom stand and all other seated in the drawing room asking questions to him. As I entered I touched the feet of Pappi's Dad and Mom. His Dad said, "Anupam *beta* see what has he done."

"What happened uncle?"

"He thinks of himself as SRK and now he's trying to be one by proposing to the girls of the neighbourhood."

"Proposing? Who did he propose and when did he propose?"

Aunty said, "Anupam at least you don't try to be naïve, you know everything."

"Aunty if you're talking about the incident which happened a few days ago, then yes I do know about it, but he didn't do it in a free will, he was under pressure by that thug."

Sehgal Uncle said, *"He is lying. Yeh baal hamne dhoop mai safed nahi kiye hai* (I know what he has done). Don't we know that in this age what all happens to guys. I am going to complain it to the Police." I couldn't stand the way he spoke and nobody moved or said a word, so I just went and stood by Pappi at the door. Sharma uncle asked Pappi to tell the truth and Pappi repeated the same story.

Pappi's mom said, "Anupam beta you tell us the truth."

I said, "Aunty Pappi is telliing the truth, I have seen that guy myself and he is a full rascal, he has friends from the slum area and anyone is bound to get frightened if someone from there threatens him and that too when he's alone." They asked Pappi's father, "Vishnu, tell us what do we do?" Uncle replied very politely, "My son is like your son, he has done a mistake and now I don't know what you should do *bhai saahab*. Do whatever you feel is right and don't worry if my son is wrong he'll have to pay for it."

Sehgal Uncle said, "Look Pappi this is the last time I'm asking you to tell the truth, and after that I won't say a single word to you." Pappi kept his patience and repeated the same thing. Hearing it Sehgal Uncle went fiery red and furious he stood up and went out and said, "I'm going to the Police."

But then Sharma uncle held him by arm and pulled him back inside the house and said, "One tight slap and your brains will be back to normal.

Are you nuts? You call me your elder brother and you are not listening to my words. If you go to the Police and once they start interrogating the matter it will be your daughter who'll get a bad name in the society, have you thought of it. Sit we can talk and discuss it out." Sehgal Uncle sat down and Sharma uncle asked him, "What do you want?"

"I want him to say sorry and promise that he won't do this again." Sehgal Uncle said. Sharma uncle then turned to his Dad and said, "See Vishnu we all know that your son is very good and we've seen him since his childhood days, but now if he has done something wrong then he has to be sorry for it, it doesn't matter if he did it under some threat or anything else."

Pappi's Dad said, "Yes I agree. Pappi say sorry to uncle and promise him that you won't repeat it."

Pappi did exactly what his Dad asked him to do, he touched Sehgal Uncle's feet and said sorry by holding his ears and also promised that this won't be repeated again. He also said sorry to his Dad and to Sharma uncle as well. At least he was able to at least prove that he's not afraid because he's right and he's saying sorry because yes it was a kind of mistake that he made.

Thanks to Sharma uncle for saving Pappi and thanks to his father who remained cool and polite in this matter and after that he didn't say a word to Pappi.

It all got over, but Pappi could never give up loving Rinki, he loved Rinki more than he loved anything, at times he felt sorry because under pressure he denied the fact that he loved her, but what was to happen had already happened. The nuke of love had already killed Pappi and Rinki. Pappi because he had triggered it off at the wrong time and had lost the first battle for the love of his life. He loved her with everything he had and everything he wished to achieve. His only objective was to marry Rinki and call her wife.

As time went and Pappi spent more time with family and friends which helped him to become normal but then ill fate struck once again. The trouble was far from over. One day at a dhaba Monu and few of his friends from the neighbourhood were having a cocktail party and a guy whose name was Deepak suddenly slipped his tongue and said, "Whatever happened to Pappi and Rinki shouldn't have happened."

Monu asked, "What happened to Rinki? My sister?" Deepak now realized that he had said something wrong under the effect of Alcohol so he said, "Naa not your sister, it was just something else." But Monu didn't let it go and kept on insisting Deepak to tell him the story and Deepak told him the whole incident.

Monu became angry and said, "I'll not leave that son of bitch tell me who was he. I'll ask Pappi and then fucking beat the hell out of him." His friends calmed him down for that instance but Monu didn't forget it.

Next day Deepak and another of his friend Ashish from the same neighbourhood took Pappi for a smoke and there they confessed about whatever they told to Monu the previous night and apologized for their slip of tongue.

Pappi said, "Now what will happen?"

Ashish said, "Don't worry we are there if Monu says something to you let us know, we will take care of him."

But Monu didn't forget and was eager to know what happened, so he asked his mother and his mother told him the whole incident.

Few days later Monu came on his bike and said, "Hi Pappi. Wassup man? How are you doing?"

"I'm good *bhaiya*."

"Chal sit will go for a smoke."

"No *Bhaiya* I don't smoke."

"Okay yaar you have tea or coffee." Pappi knew that something is wrong but he couldn't refuse as his denial would mean that even he's the culprit and that might trigger of Monu psycho anger. So he went with Monu to a dhaba. They ordered two glasses of tea. Monu lit a King Size Gold Flake and by the time tea came he started, "Pappi yaar I love my sister Rinki."

Pappi said, "I know *bhaiya*, every brother loves his sister."

"Yaar Pappi, I can do anything for her. I have picked up lots of fight for her and beaten lots of guys too." '*Saala Psycho*' thought Pappi and said, "*Right Bhaiya* you did the right thing. These kinds of guys should be beaten."

He then said "Yaar I heard that even you had some issues with Rinki." Pappi maintained his calm and cool and said, "*Yes bhaiya*."

"What happened, tell me."

"*Bhaiya* what's the point in digging up old issues, whatever happened can't be changed, everything is back to normal now and I've forgotten everything and I request you to forget them as well."

"Tell me, who was that asshole that threatened you to propose my sister?"

Pappi now gave a real ass saving diplomatic answer, "*Bhaiya* see there are a lot of idiots roaming around a beautiful girl, and Rinki is also beautiful so there must be hundreds like him, how many can we pick up a fight with. It was him who did it this time. Next time he would get it done through his friends, we can't just keep picking up fights with everyone. We will surely take care of him if he tries something like this for the next time." Monu was convinced by this and said, "Yes Pappi you are absolutely right, I respect you and I keep telling everyone that guys should be like Pappi." This relieved Pappi. After this conversation they returned back and Pappi thanked heavens for saving his butt once more from getting kicked.

Came January and it was time for the festival of Lohri. It was celebrated at Rinki's house since they were Punjabis and every family of his neighbourhood participated in that. That year every one from Pappi's family went to the Sehgal's. There Sehgal Uncle hugged his father and said, "You are my brother. How are you?" 'Brother huh! Brother my ass thought Pappi. Sehgal Uncle said, "I've forgot all sad and sorry memories and I hope even you have." Pappi's father was also very happy now. Pappi didn't go to the function as he felt too ashamed to be there, even the love for Rinki couldn't break his shame. At the function everyone was standing near the sacred fire of Lohri and were revolving around it, dancing, but Pappi was at home, suddenly he heard someone yelling his name, as he went out he saw Monu. Monu said, "Harshit said you were not coming for the Lohri celebration.

Why bro, just forget everything and come celebrate with us."

Pappi went with him to the celebration but Sehgal Uncle was still annoyed with Pappi as he didn't answer Pappi's *Namaste* and turned his face off Pappi, but Sehgal Aunty was very humble and said, "Namaste beta. How are you?"

"I'm okay Aunty." Just then he saw Rinki and he smiled at her and said, "Hi." She too smiled at him; once again the smile killed Pappi and sent him to the heaven of love. That evening he laughed, chatted and danced with Rinki just like the old days and his love for Rinki grew by leaps and bounds that evening. Slowly everyone forgot this incident but still down the memory lane it gets recalled sometimes by Pappi as a sweet memory and the proposal to the girl he loved, and still loves.

Loving someone is not a crime even if Pappi promised Sehgal Uncle that he would not do it again but it was sure that he would never accept that he's defeated and this incident gave him a spark to become something in life. He took a vow to be an achiever and do whatever it takes to call Rinki as his wife, but this time only with more courage, achievement, dignity and with the resolution that this time the nuke of love won't kill love.

16

MATHEMATICS

Don't Touch Him Sir!

Rinki's incident left Pappi in wreck but with time that incident also made him stronger and made him understand love. The ambience in the classroom was always that of fun and frolic, that helped Pappi slowly come back to normal. The guys all the time were in mood for fun especially during the lecture of Mathematics. The lecturer was Mr. Mathur nicknamed as Mathura Prasad by the batch.

Mr. Mathur was an old man probably must have been in his late fifties. He wore thick spectacles the power of which was unknown, but the guesses of students ranged anywhere from +/- 10 to +/- 100, whatever must have been the power but surely it was a degree of power without which

Mr. Mathur went blind. In classroom whenever he was teaching with his back towards the students, the boys would start a 'chalk war' which was fought with pieces of chalk. Each one of the rows would become a team and then the massive chalk war would start. Few of the chalk bullets would also hit the blackboard right besides Mr. Mathur. He always ignored them. Needless to mention that the noise in the classroom was deafening, most of which was composed of students yelling out the word chai or tea as the tea vendors in railway station do it. It sounded somewhat like '*ey chaaay, piyo garam chaaay.*' I don't have a clue from where this chaaay culture came up but it was fun. Even the girls of the classroom enjoyed that fun.

One day while the usual noisy Mathematics lecture was going on Mr. Mathur unable to control his temperament yelled back, "Why the hell do you guys make such hell of a noise. The Principal would think that I have no control over the class. If you boys do not understand anything that I teach then you are free to take out your own Mathematics books of course or competitive exams and solve them. But please keep some silence in the class and don't disturb my concentration." As soon as Mr. Mathur finished his statement and turned back to the blackboard the talk of the town was Mr. Mathur's concentration. Although for the remaining duration of the lecture the class remained quiet as compared to the previous lectures.

But this peace of class was limited only to that particular lecture. After that the situation was switched back to normal and Mr. Mathur was also back to normal. My gang didn't attend the Mathematics lecture for probably next two weeks.

If I remember correctly it was Thursday, the only day when the lab practicals where in the first half and the second half was for theory classes. There were three lectures to be attended in the second half and two out of them were Mr. Mathur's lectures. That day we were so unlucky that we couldn't run away from School and got stuck up with the lecture.

As usual the class was on top of its voice. As Mr. Mathur entered the classroom the guys started hooting as if some famous movie star has entered the class. A voice from the back benches came, "Sir you looking cool and handsome today." The whole of the class laughed like hell at this. Mr. Mathur looked in good mood that day, he replied, "Well, I'm always handsome boys my days of youth were more killing." The girls giggled at this and the boys roared into laughter. I took the last seat of the middle row, took out my FIITJEE Mathematics test booklet of integral calculus and started solving the problems. The class as usual was having chalk war with active participation from Pappi and others. All of a sudden from the last benches of the row on my left a missile of chalk flew and it landed direct on the back of Mr. Mathur. The whole class was stunned to silence by that. Mr. Mathur turned back and his face clearly stated that he was very upset by that. He asked, “Who threw that thing on my back?” as soon as he asked the question the whole of the class burst into giggling laughter. This infuriated him even more. I looked up and all the class was laughing in giggles I saw the look of Mr. Mathur’s face and I couldn’t stop myself from breaking into laughter. He looked like a crack pot of sixty year old who is confused and and does not know what to do and shouts all around the place. He walked up to me with the duster in his hand and swung his hand right across to hit me with the duster. In my self-defence I just put my right hand up in the air, his swinging hand was blocked by my right hand and the duster in his hand fell. Damn! It fell and it fell right on his toe. This made his anger grow by quantum leaps.

He yelled, “Stand up you idiot. What do you think of yourself, you will do whatever you want in the class and break the discipline of the class? I will take disciplinary action against you, you come with me to the Principal.” as I stood up he looked at me. I was quite tall for him so he looked at me as if he is looking at some giant.

I said, "What did I do sir?"

"You threw a chalk at me."

"Prove it." This reply of mine made the whole class stun to silence and Mr. Mathur too.

I continued, "First of all you can't control the class. Second no one understands what you teach in the class. Third someone else throws a chalk at you and you come and try to hit the wrong boy, who is solving his own Mathematics problems for IIT/JEE. You want to take me to the Principal, okay let's go; I will tell him what you said in the class two weeks ago. It was you who said that if we are unable to understand your teaching in the class we can solve our own Mathematics questions and here I'm trying to solve some integral calculus questions and you blame me for hitting you with a damn chalk. That is ridiculous." Mr. Mathur went on the backfoot hearing this reply from me.

He said, "I must have mistaken, you can sit down." He picked up the duster and started to walk back to the board. As he was walking back Pappi stood up from the last bench of the row from where the chalk came and said, *"Sir usko haath mat lagana, theek nahi hoga* (Sir, don't you dare touch him, won't be good for you)" This made the whole class look at Pappi and me. I looked at him and gave him the 'why did you have to jump in between idiot' look. As Pappi sat down Mr. Mathur reached the blackboard and addressed the class, "There are some good students in the class who study, but at times if we say anything to them by mistake they should understand. Even teachers are humans and can make mistakes. They are good students and should continue concentrating on their good efforts." This statement of Mr. Mathur made the whole class burst into laughter.

Later when the Mathematics lecture was over we bunked the remaining lecture and at the tapri I said to Pappi, "What the fuck you think you were doing in the class? Why did you stand up and say that to Mathura."

"*Arre yaar* he was trying to beat you for no fault of yours. How could I tolerate that someone would hit my brother like that."

"Okay dude I understand but then what if he would have dragged us to the Principal. We already had a good meeting with him if you remember."

"So what, this time we were on the right side and I was on my bro's side. I wouldn't have cared a fuck."

"Okay bro." I could feel what he felt and I hugged him.

That evening I didn't go to coaching so I couldn't see Abhishikta, but for friends it was worth it. That night when I sat down to study I dragged my pen with an unconscious mind scribbling answers to a physics problem; I was lost in her thoughts completely. When I looked at the notebook I saw the most beautiful name in my life that I could ever see it read 'Abhishikta'. That night I did nothing just to play F.L.A.M.E.S. with her name and see that name inscribed on my notebook. I don't remember when I fell asleep. But the dream that night I will never forget. That dream was my perfect dream of marriage with Abhishikta. As I entered the hotel room she said, "Anupam I love you, this honeymoon will be the most memorable days of our life. Just look at the spectacular silhouettes of the silvery mountains while the full moon showers the rays of silver."

She was spangled in beautiful blue saree with golden embroidery. I kissed her forehead and said, "Please keep showering your silver rays of love on me for the rest of my life." and we hugged each other tightly. That was the best wifey hug a husband could ever get. I felt so lucky I continued to her, "It's more than me saying you're beautiful. It's more factual than saying I first saw you in a crowded road. It's true that you're beautiful, and I have always seen about these beautiful moments:

'The portrait of a woman in her essence when I saw you I fell in love with you.'

'Found in the wild, was an innocent face with the moistest lips the softness of which I felt when I kissed you.'

'Your face playing hide and seek like a beautiful butterfly in black and bright red with your deep black beautiful silky hair."' We embraced each other with our lips locked and souls making love. We gave in to the flow of emotion and passion. I hugged my wife with the most firm grip, like a kid sleeping in utmost comfort and care hugs its teddy bear tightly. THUD!

'Damn why the bed is so hard like concrete' I thought. TRAAANNNN! TRAAANNNN! The alarm clock went off. Damn! Hell, the most beautiful night of my life, the most beautiful moment of my life was a dream with the love of my life as my wife. I got up, shut off the alarm clock, freshened up and moved out for my regular football practice.

17

FAREWELL

School Of Dreams

Soon February ended and came the month of March. It was the last month for all of us at the School of our dreams. End of all the fun of two years, end of all bunking of classes, friends teasing me about Rekha, smoking at the woods and at the Habibganj railway station. Every thing was coming to an end. We had to part our ways with those friends with whom we had spent the most glorious two years of our life, friends with whom we had fought, friends with whom we had bunked classes, friends who had given proxy attendance for us when we bunked classes, friends who lend us Rs. 2.50 when we needed it for a *WILLS NAVY CUT* cigarette, friends who would pull us when our bikes ran out of gas, friends who helped us cheat in the exams, friends who covered our asses up when we messed up in the Chemistry labs and friends who did what not for us. We had to part our ways with those people who taught us the true feeling of friendship. What it means to live for a friend and to die for a friend, with the only exception of when I was stabbed in the back by a friend and I lost Abhishikta forever from my life.

The day of our farewell was disclosed to us which officially would be the last day of us at School.

It was a Wednesday for our farewell and we decided to meet up at Pappi's place and then move on from there to the School. I dressed up quite casually in formals, picked up my Hero Puch and headed off straight for Pappi's home. On the way my bike stopped with few jerks. I kicked my bike, but the bike didn't start. 'Damn what's the fucking problem with you?' I roared in my thoughts. After five minutes of terrible kicking my legs started to pain but the bike didn't start. I put the bike on main stand and opened the fuel tank lid and Yo! What a fucking luck, not just my luck but even my bike had run out of petrol. I was stuck up with a dry bike from where the nearest petrol pump was almost four kilometres away. 'Thank You GOD!' I thought. In those days I used to be believer. Pushing my bike for 4 kilometres and drenched in sweat I reached the petrol pump and Yo! The petrol pump was dry. ‘What a fucking luck. Today’s luck for me must have been written using an asses disk.’ In shear disappointment I sat there cursing my luck. Then I spotted a tyre puncture repair shop about 100 meters away.

I went and asked, “Bhaiya petrol milega kya.”

The owner of the shop said, “Kitna Chhaiye?”

“Ek litre”

“Paintees Rupees”

‘What the fuck petrol of twenty two Rupees per litre being sold at thirty five Rupees per litre, its pure black marketing.’ But I had no other option so I gave him thirty five Rupees for a litre of petrol which was at least 45% V/V adulterated with kerosene. I filled my bike with that I gave it a few more kicks and it roared again although the effect of the adulterated fuel was audible. After the engine roared into action I headed straight for Pappi’s home, but the group had already left after much waiting. Upon reaching School I saw the gang outside School, I joined them. All of them were well dressed especially Pappi, he was looking handsome and was all set to win the Mr. Handsome award for the day. The function began with the address of Mishra Sir; our function began by making a circular seating arrangement out of the row arrangements. By the time Mishra Sir finished his speech we had started the game '*Chidiya Udd'* (fly bird), well it's tough to explain the game here. Anyways by the time speeches finished we had flown most of the teachers in the game.

Brijesh Patel the ace Maths teacher came and said, "What are you 12th 'B' guys flying today." We said in unison, "Nothing Sir." As soon as he left we did '*Brijesh Patel Udd'* (Brijesh Patel, fly). Then the most important announcement of the function came from Vajpayee, "boys of 12th 'B' could you guys please leave the function and please rejoin the function again for lunch. The girls can stay back."

This was an insult so we walked right out of the function through the stage. At the parking we decided that something had to be done for this insult. One of our guys had some Diwali crackers, the ones we call '*Rassi Bomb'*. We decided to place them at the four corners of the School, one in the girls' toilet, one near the Principal's room and one near the stage.

The fuses were set so that the crackers would explode almost at the same time. The bombs went off in an order which no one thought of, first the corners of the School gave the sound then the one near Principal's office and girls' toilet, immediately after that the one near the stage went off, the whole function came to a stand still and we sped off from the parking. Everyone knew that 12th 'B' was responsible for it, but no one could catch us or prove it. We ran from School even on the last day, but then today no one stopped us, or no one was following us. This was strange, we were accustomed to teachers following us or Paramlal trying to stop us and today when no one did that we felt that our School lives have come to an end. Once we sped off from School we went to *Bajrang* Dairy in Indrapuri, a famous sweet shop. Coke and Pepsi bottles were opened like champagne bottles and the cola was sprayed high in the air and on the shirts of everyone. Feasting on *samosas and kachoris* we were dancing and singing on the main road right in front of Bajrang Dairy which resulted in a total traffic jam. For almost 15 minutes we kept the traffic blocked. We were so absorbed in the celebration that none of us noticed that the traffic was blocked. After a blasting party at Bajrang Dairy we returned back to School. By the time lunch was already served, but after the party at Bajrang none of us were in the mood to have lunch. We decided to head straight to our classroom. As we entered a strange feeling of being stranger to a known classroom gripped us. As we took our seats, no one said anything, perhaps the classroom we all had proudly said to be our own had by now declared us to be strangers and was now waiting for the new batch. I wondered how many such batches this Classroom had seen. None of us spoke, all of us had moist eyes. I thought, 'was this the same class 12th 'B'?' 'Were these the same boys whom all the teachers and even the Principal had considered to be the menace of the School?' 'Was this the same class which was declared to be rank one in School's blacklist?' 'No! Definitely no, today what I saw was a group of boys who were getting separated from their friends; best friends and none of them knew when they would be able to see them again in life.' Before the tears would have rolled out we decided to click some snaps in smiling faces; and what better place than the walls which were used to escape from that golden School. We all marched towards the wall which we used most commonly to escape from School. While moving towards the wall, again the feeling of being a stranger crept in, today there was no Paramlal to run behind us, or no Vajpayee to run with a scooter behind us, we were freely allowed to go up to the wall climb on it and click snaps. Everything changed so suddenly.

We finally said our goodbyes, hugged each other with tears in our eyes and the promise that we would meet each other whenever it's possible in life.

Board Exams:

Our board exams started and" on the day of chemistry exam"

On the day of Chemistry exam, I took a camera with me to the School; of course a borrowed one. Soon I met Pappi, Abhishek and Rana. We took out our vehicles I got the idea of clicking snaps in our School uniform which we didn't have. We got out of the School campus and parked out vehicles by roadside and clicked a couple of photographs, which became the best photographs of my life. Even today those photographs make me feel like I'm standing there on that road, with my best friend, just finished our board exams and will be together forever in life.

But when the reality strikes back, it pains much more than what it hurt when I left the School to make our progress in careers, I would not say life, because even after 10 years my life hasn't progressed a bit, still waiting for Abhishikta to come back in my life, still waiting to be with my best friend, fight with him, drink with him, roam around the city with him, chase girls with him. The last 10 years have given a bit of career and success in life, have travelled to some of the most developed countries on this planet but that doesn't bring smile on my face, that doesn't soothe my heart, doesn't give me a sense of protection like my best friend gave me, when didn't have any of this money, career or professional success. It makes me feel like UNTITLED.

18

RESULTS: SAGA OF SUCCESS, FAILURES

And The Determination To Try Again

It was month of May when the results started pouring in. It started with the M.P Board declaring the 12th standard results. I got a call from Pappi that the results were out, so I went to his home to pick him up and from there we went directly to board office where the results were displayed on the notice board.

I asked Pappi to go with my roll number and check out the results. Not because that I wasn't confident about the result, in fact I was very confident about my results. I just didn't want to enter the chaotic crowd in the campus who were all gathered around the notice board and seemed like all had participated in a multi–player wrestling competition.

Pappi's main aim being the board exams he couldn't wait to see the results, he rushed and pushed his way through the crowd. After several minutes he came out of the crowd and rushed towards me, the glow in his face told me that he had done quite well in the exams. He came to me and said, "*O kaake*, I have scored above 77% in the exams and Maths it's 91 out of 100." Well let me clear one thing first, we were never the topper material, I know there are students who have scored 99% in 12th exams, but then they probably never had fun like we did.

When we calculated the exact percentage obtained by Pappi, it was a figure which was a total disbelief for us, the figure was 77.33%; exactly the number given by the soul when we did Planchette. I felt very happy for him; I too had scored quite well with distinction in physics. It was a relief for us that we had cleared our 12th board exams.

Later that night Pappi was filled with tears when he was alone on the roof terrace of his home and cursing himself for being in such a hurry to propose Rinki and everything turning out to be a cataclysm. He wished only if he had waited for three four months and wished her in the month of March, he would have probably won her heart and today she would have been with her. But now all that was left was a set of moist eyes for him. He decided to work hard, very hard and turn the tables around and this time he would get Rinki.

A few days later the results of various engineering competitive exams started coming out and none of the boys from my group including me was able to crack any of the exams. It was absolute disappointment for me. I decided to give it a try once again.

Pappi's career was a bit uncertain. Under the jeopardy of ruining a year he was advised by his Dad either to take up a B.Sc course in computers or like me take a year's drop and prepare whole heartedly for the engineering competitive exams. But Pappi's mind was in a qualm as he did not want to take B.Sc course in computers nor he had the confidence of clearing the MPPET exam leave aside the IIT/JEE exam.

Pappi's maternal uncle or mamaji who was P.A. or personal assistant to State Education Minister at that time, and was having a good hold at the engineering colleges wanted him to pursue Polytechnic from SATI Vidisha as he had lot of lecturers and the registrar known to him and he told me that he will try to get a good result for him and after that he would get him admission in second year of (Bachelor of Engineering) (B.E.) in MACT. This looked like a sound plan for Pappi.

After a series of family discussions, it was decided for teenaged Pappi that he would go on to study diploma in computers from SATI Vidisha. One of the major reasons for Pappi agreeing to this was that Rinki took a B.Com course, the course was a three year course, after which Rinki would be married off to some idiot by her parents. So Pappi had these three years to prove his worth and stop the upcoming dreadful event which would take everything away from him.

So within a week Pappi's journey to success in life as a software engineer begun with the daily travel from Bhopal to Vidisha. Faced with furious and insane kind of ragging he started the journey to success.

One day one of the seniors of Pappi, Rajesh Pendam asked him to go to a senior girl named Seema and ask her height. Pappi was tensed but he was threatened that if he doesn't do it then he would face the consequences in train during the returning journey.

Pappi went to Seema, greeted her with Good Morning madam. Pappi was looking down as it was not healthy custom to look into the eyes of seniors. Seema replied, “Good Morning Aayush."

"Madam how do you know my name?"

“You are here since four days and every one knows you.” Pappi was eased at this.

“Do not be shy and clearly say what it is that you want?”

"Madam what is your height?"

She asked him to call her Seema but Pappi said that she was his senior and he should not call her by her name but she insisted that as both were of same age so he should call her by name. So Pappi again asked her "Seema what is your height?"

Seema looking at Pappi’s innocence said “It’s five feet three inches.”

Next day another senior asked Pappi to go to another senior girl named Shweta to ask for her Maths notebook for couple of days. Pappi went to her and said "Good morning Madam."

She replied "Good morning Aayush.” Again Pappi was surprised that she too knew his name. Like Seema she too insisted to call her by her name. Pappi said "Good morning Shweta."

She was happy about it and replied, “Yes Aayush what is it that you need?”

“I want your Maths notebook for two days.”

“Ok take it.” She gave him her notebook.

Pappi went to the senior and gave him the notebook Rajesh was also standing there. He asked Pappi, "What do you say to the girls you bugger.”

Pappi replied, “Sir whatever you ask me to do.”

“Dude I can’t see what is the charm of this idiot. No girl has ever told us their height or given their Maths notebook. Maybe it’s because he looks innocent and handsome.”

The jealousy of the seniors was increasing day by day and Pappi knew that something disastrous will happen very soon.

Few days later during the journey back to Bhopal some senior girls asked Pappi to sit with them as they wanted his complete introduction. The other juniors were sitting in the other compartment with the senior boys. One senior madam asked him to tell about his own self. Pappi gave the typical technical introduction in Hindi, which is a trademark for all technical institutions in MP.

After that Pappi was made to sit in between the senior girls that meant now on either side of Pappi were girls and all were staring at him.

One of them asked him to sing a song for her. Pappi asked, “Which song?”

She said, "Any song from the latest movie you have seen."

Pappi sang the song '*Ek din aap yun ham ko mil jayenge*' from another damn SRK movie. Pappi could never let go off SRK, I never knew why. After he finished all the girls applauded and congratulated him on singing well and said that he sings quite well. The sound of clapping didn't stop even after a long time Pappi saw that the girls have already stopped clapping. Then Pappi realized that the sound was not of clapping it was the sound of slapping. The senior boys have started the ragging in the train and the junior boys were getting slapped. The senior girls got worried and one of them Neelam Singh said, "Girls we have to do something to save him from all that inhumane torture."

Another girl said, "Aayush you continue singing songs." Pappi continued on songs one after another. One of the seniors came to them and asked the girls to hand Pappi over to them as the senior boys were calling him but the girls told him that they are ragging him now, once they finish then only Pappi will go to them.

To save him from ragging they kept on asking him to perform one or the other thing. Pappi was also good in mimicry so he performed that as well in front of the girls. Neelam then asked him that if he had to propose her, how he will do that. Now this was something very easy for Pappi as Pappi was a Bollywood movie freak and he now got a chance to act in front of them. Neelam was surprised to see his acting talent. Pappi managed to bring tears in his eyes while performing that act and tears are a superb act for girls whether they perform it or someone performs it for them. Pappi was thinking of Rinki and Neelam thought that he is really proposing her and she said 'yes'. The moment she said 'yes' everybody started laughing. Then she realized that it was all an act. Even Pappi was shocked by this act of her's. All this drama saved Pappi's ass that day. Upon reaching Bhopal, one of the seniors asked him to have cigarette, Pappi denied. The guy said if Pappi doesn't smoke here and later on if he saw Pappi smoking elsewhere then he will beat the fuck out of him. Pappi realized that being a good person will do no good to him and he took the cigarette from him and started smoking. The way he was smoking, the senior asked him, "You are a chain smoker aren't you." Pappi said, "Yes sir." He then told him that today he was saved somehow but tomorrow they will make sure that you get double.

The second day also it happened the same way and the senior girls saved Pappi's ass from getting spanked. This angered the seniors even more as they were not getting hold of him at the same time Pappi was gaining popularity with the girls.

The third day after reaching Vidisha the seniors instead of going to college took Pappi to a nearby Chai tapri to have morning snacks as the train reached a lot early than the expected time.

Rajesh said, "You are really very handsome and smart boy. Look at the kind of response you get from the girls in our college. You can have any girl as your girlfriend. Yes or No?"

"No"

"No" WHACK! And Pappi got one tight slap from one of them. Rajesh continued, "Listen you bugger if you want to stay in this college you need to be confident and you need to be proactive. I'm telling you that you can impress any girl I have the confidence in you then why don't you have confidence in yourself."

"Because I already tried once and the result was heartbreaking for me so I just don't want to try again." The seniors kept on slapping him. At last just to save himself from getting further slaps Pappi told them yes he can. Things changed that very moment and one of the seniors said, "Okay so tomorrow you are going to propose a girl and make her your girlfriend."

Pappi said, "Sir if any problem rises then what?"

They said, “Don’t worry we will handle you just propose a girl.” Pappi agreed.

Later that evening while returning from Vidisha Pappi’s luck ran out of fuel and he got into the hands of the senior boys.

Pappi was getting slapped but he didn’t cry. Today when he recalls that day, he says, “I don’t know what happened to me that day. They beat me for almost 15 minutes every senior was eager to damage my face it was with a mixed feeling of jealousy and the other thing was I was getting saved from last 2 days so I got more slaps from them. But I didn’t cry.” Bhopal station was about to come and when they realized that, they gave him a comb to set his hair right and asked him to wash the face. Pappi washed his face but the marks of slaps were still visible on his cheeks as they became red. Pappi returned to his home and slept, his mother and father realized that something wrong did happen and they went to him but Pappi was so tired and didn’t want to show his face to parents so he asked them to go and sleep. He also told them that he had snacks at the station canteen sponsored by seniors so he is not hungry. But his mother took his head in her lap and saw his face. Instantly the tears of pain for her son started rolling down her cheeks, she cried. His father too became very angry at first he thought that Pappi had a fight with someone, but when Pappi told them everything. His father told him that the next day he is going to come with him to Vidisha. Pappi said, “This is going to be a daily routine Dad, so don’t worry after 3-4 months this ragging will stop. I will manage its ok as it happens to everyone.” Pappi was a guy with lots of guts so his father knew that it will be okay. Few days later his mamaji came on *Rakshabandhan* (Hindu festival that celebrates the love and duty between brothers and sisters) and told him that after two days there is going to be a counselling based on 12th class marks for some new engineering colleges that are opening soon. It came as good news for Pappi and he agreed to attend the counselling. When Pappi attended the counselling he got admission in IPS Academy and that too in B.E Computer Science branch. This opened the door of even much better career prospects for him.

Pappi took admission and promised himself that he will study hard, will score good marks and make his father feel proud and will work hard to get Rinki's attention towards me. Thus began his journey to become a successful senior software engineer at HSBC. But the journey had just began and with that the hardships too.

19

CLIMAX: TURN OF

Life For Pappi

Well I don't know why I called this chapter Climax. Pappi always wanted to have a story which has a Climax and upon his request this chapter is named Climax. His Bollywood freaked out mind wants to have something in filmy *ishtyle*.

Pappi joined IPS Academy for his B.E in Computer science. I started a fresh year, well a drop year, in short I was wasting an academic year of my life. This time I wanted to clear the entrance exams, come what may. Well that didn't include Abhishikta. I got admission in Joe's classes. The day admission results for the coaching were to be announced, I went with Shekar to the coaching centre. The list was there already, as I scrolled down the list, I found my name. Wow! And am I not dreaming! Right below my name was the name written Abhishikta. I couldn't believe my eyes. Was this some kind of chemical imbalance in my mind, just because I was so much in love with Abhishikta?

That night I just wished that Abhishikta too joins the coaching. Today I wish if on that night I had wished Abhishikta marries me, life would have been different, because that night's wish was granted.

A week later I reached the classes I saw Abhishikta standing at the parking with her friends. That was the moment I knew I would screw up my entrance exams.

One fine day while returning from the coaching I banged my Hero Puch into a Maruti 800. Well it was not my fault. I was following Abhishikta as usual. Shekar was my pillion, and he kept saying drive fast dude she's getting away. Abhishikta had a Kinetic Honda, a good 100cc two stroke powerful machine which could outperform any vehicle in its class. I overtook Abhishikta, while overtaking was just staring at her, then I slowed down again and let her pass so that I can again stare at the most beautiful face in the world. As she crossed I again pulled the throttle, suddenly she switched lanes and I couldn't see the Maruti 800 in the way and that son of a bitch slammed his brakes right in the middle of the road. BANG! BOOM! I went dashing with all the momentum into the rear bumper of the car. My Hero Puch crashed I went off flying in the air and over the handle of my bike I came on the road, fraction of seconds later Shekar came flying all over on me and fraction of second later the bike fell on us. The car owner rushed off. Abhishikta crossed watching us with a sorry look on her face. As we got up Shekar said, “Let’s get out of here quick.”

“How?” I said.

Shekar gave me a puzzled look. I pointed him towards the front wheel of my bike. The circular rim of the wheel had converted into a square frame or I should say a square wheel.

Shekar said, “Oh! fuck What the hell?”

“Yes fuck the hell.”

That evening My Dad was fuming at me for the accident and I had no option but to listen to his morale breaking taunts and scoffs at me. I couldn’t even eat that night. The next day morning I was limping, my ankle was hurt badly. Shekar came to pick me up on his scooter. When we reached the coaching I saw Abhishikta parking her Kinetic.

I went to her and said, “Hi.”

She said, “Hi!”

"I have a request for you."

"Can you please speak in Hindi or English I don't understand Bengali." Bloody hell! I just made a fun out of me right in front of her. Till that day I always thought she was a Bengali because of her last name. But she was an Oriya.

I said, "Oh! Sorry" and I repeated in English.

"Yes, sure dear. Go ahead." That was so soothing for my ears I went numb and I fumbled, "Please don't tell about yesterday's incident to Joshi sir."

"Which incident?" She said that so cutely like an innocent baby. I gave her a puzzled look as if saying 'how can you forget that?'

She then realized and said, "Oh! That accident. How are you? Hope you are not hurt much. Yes I won't mention it, but why?"

"I'm good, with a sprain in my ankle. Well if you tell Joe sir about it, he will be mad at us and I don't want that."

"Don't worry dear I won't tell him, but you take care of yourself." Ahh! I just fainted hearing the word 'dear' filled with so much of care and that smile killed me almost instantaneously. As I watched her go into the building I was sure my entrance exams are screwed, but I also knew that she is the one I would be in love forever.

One fine day when I was at Shekar's home studying, he came up with a brilliant fucked up idea to bring me close to Abhishikta. I had no clue that this was the first time when his idea would wreck my day and Abhishikta's too.

He said, "Dude, Abhishikta goes to the Chemistry class every morning."

"Yes I know that, so?" I was confused.

"You don't see the point, every morning her Kinetic is parked outside the coaching."

"So you expect her to take the Kinetic with her inside the class. Idiot!"

"No yaar, I mean her Kinetic is parked for almost two hours without any guard."

I said, "Okay so you want me to be a guard for her Kinetic. Dude listen I want to be her guard for life, not for her Kinetic."

"Oh! Hell, I'm not asking you to guard her Kinetic. See if one fine morning, when she comes out of the Chemistry class and finds her Kinetic has a flat tyre." This was getting interesting.

Shekar continued, "She will need help to take care of the flat tyre and herself. If that help comes in your form, then she spends half a day with you and some coffee, wow! So romantic."

I didn't like this freaked out plan, but the greed of spending half a day with Abhishikta played on my mind.

The next day I went at the Chemistry coaching I spotted her silver Kinetic with the exact number plate on it. I slowly pulled up my bike behind her Kinetic. I intentionally threw the tyre flattening equipment kit down. I took the divider in my hand and stabbed it hard into the rear tyre of the Kinetic, nothing happened. I pulled the divider back from the tyre, fuck! The rounder came out but only with one needle, the other needle stuck right there. It was like abandoning a lunar module on the surface of moon after the mission was over. Just then I heard the sound 'hisssss'. Magnitude of the sound was increasing so I rushed off from there. Now I had almost one and a half hour to kill before the coaching would be over and I get to spend the rest of the day with Abhishikta. I spent around 1 hour and 15 minutes at Habibganj railway station, going through my physics assignments and smoking NAVY Cut. I started off from there hoping to see Abhishikta; helping her with the flat tyre and then spending the day with her at a good coffee shop. The mere thought of it was so mesmerizing and romantic for me. I reached the coaching; I knew where to look for Abhishikta. But I couldn't see there. It was then I realized that the coaching class had finished fifteen minutes earlier than the regular time. Shit! And there was Abhishikta talking and walking with some other guy. FUCKING HELL!!! Just then I saw Shekar.

He came to me and said, “Where the hell were you?”

I said, “I thought the class would be over in 1 and half hours?”

“Okay but now go and help Abhishikta.”

“Have you seen her?”

“No.” Shekar said. I pointed him towards Abhishikta.

Shekar said, “shit! What is he doing with her?”

“Who is he?” I was furious.

“Abhishek. My classmate.” I was so depressed. We headed off from there; I was so utterly disappointed that time. That day Abhishikta didn’t come to class.

That evening I called her, her sister picked up the phone “Hello!”

I said, “Hello, can I speak to Abhishikta please? This is Anupam.”

“Hold on please.”

Then she yelled ‘Eina there is a call for you.’ Abhishikta came and asked, “Who is it?”

Her sister replied “Anupam. Isn’t he the same guy who punctured your Kinetic today morning?”

“Shut up! He didn’t do anything. He doesn’t even know what happened, go now.” I was so relieved.

She said, “Hello!” and casted her spell on me. I once again went numb.

“Hello.”

“Hi Anupam.”

“Hi, how are you?” I was nervous.

“I’m fine.”

“I didn’t see you today morning at the class, so got worried about you and called up. Why didn’t you come today at the coaching?”

“Actually my Kinetic had a flat tyre, so couldn’t come.”

“Oh! Is it so? Where at your home? Someone could have dropped you.”

“No not at my home at the Chemistry class.”

“Oh! I didn’t know that, or else I would have helped you.”

“Thank you so much for being nice.”

“So will I be seeing you tomorrow?”

“Of course you will be.”

"Wow great."

That was the day when for the first time I had believed in somebody else's idea and lost out.

By the end of the year 2000 I was lucky enough to have got through to MACT or Maulana Azad College of Technology, the best engineering college in the state and one of the best REC's or Regional Engineering colleges in the country. I was so happy because now I could have a career, good salary, and eventually the ultimate nirvana - Abhishikta as my wife. I had started building dreams of life with Abhishikta, marrying Eina, having a good and beautiful life with Eina. But those were my dreams, which would never get fulfilled.

While time flew all these years, Pappi was doing his engineering. Every time he called me he cried a lot. He was depressed and lonely, the only thing left in his life was Rinki as in my life was Abhishikta. He was really in love with Rinki.

Pappi was in his final year of engineering and the final semester was going on when I told him that Rinki's wedding has being fixed and she will be getting married the next year around December.

I could tell from his voice that his dreams shattered and he was in severe depression. But I told him to concentrate on his exams as he had to appear in ten theory and twelve practical exams to attend due to backlogs.

It was real hard and tough for Pappi to do that, but he is a real fighter. He finished his engineering and came back to Bhopal.

The man getting married to Rinki was a baldy and fatso and looked a lot elder than Rinki. Rinki and he made no match.

Next day I asked Pappi, "You told me once that Rinki and Arti are good friends. Lets have a talk with her to enquire about what Rinki thinks about this marriage and what she thinks about you." Rinki and Arti were good friends but the friendship was almost forgotten when Rinki changed her School. They didn't meet after that.

Pappi said, "But why will Arti help us to talk to Rinki. Arti loves me and she expects that I will come to her one day. You know buddy girls have one common quality of jealousy for other girls. They feel whatever is mine should be mine it should not go to someone else."

I said, "Girls also have one more quality that when they love someone they can do anything for the person they love."

"But I'm not going to talk to her."

"Ok I will do that but how can we get her number."

"Pinky has her number."

Pappi got Arti's number from Pinky and passed it on to me.

I called Arti and asked her to meet up and told her that this is regarding Pappi. She agreed but Pappi was damn sure that she might be expecting something else thinking that Pappi is interested in her.

I said, "Yes I know that and let her think that way because that is the reason that she will come and meet us otherwise she would have never come to meet us."

Pappi and I went to children's park. Arti came and as soon as she saw Pappi she hugged him tightly.

Her eyes were moist "Pappi! Finally I'm able to meet you. I'm crazy about you and I always thought that you will never take the initiative and tell me about your feelings."

"Arti I think you are taking it the wrong way." Pappi tried to clear things.

"I Love You." She was persistent.

"Arti I have spent a very good time with you and I love those memories but to be honest with you, I see you as a best friend and nothing more than that." These words were like Kamikaze for Arti.

Pappi continued, “Arti please take everything in a good spirit, I hate myself whenever I make anyone feel bad.” She started crying and that made Pappi nervous. He stared at me. I went away but I gestured him to comfort Arti.

Pappi sat down with Arti and took her hands in his hand kissed her palms and said "Arti we don’t know when and how we fall in love, but when we do the past life is erased from our memories and if at all they exist, then they exist as good memories. It doesn’t matter whether she loves me or not but I love her and that is my commitment to her. I can only say sorry to you that I’m turning down a girl who is crazy about me and loves me so much that I felt like a celebrity star when you hugged me.”

These words brought floods in Arti’s eyes she said, "Pappi right from the day I met you I loved you. But I guess every human on this planet doesn’t get love."

Pappi said, "Ok so now you have grown up. Good to know this."

Hearing this she slapped him softly on his cheeks and said, “You will never change and again she hugged him.”

When I saw them smiling again I knew everything was back to normal and I went to them and said, “Arti don’t be sad I’m there you can love me if you want to.”

At made all of us roar into laughter and released the tension of the situation.

I said, "Arti I want a favour from you for your sweet Pappi."

"Tell me I'm ready to do anything and everything for Pappi." Her tone had the slight sound of melancholy.

"Pappi is in love with Rinki your friend from his neighbourhood. He proposed her 4 years ago, but the proposal was turned down by Rinki at that time. Now she is getting married to some uncle type guy and Pappi wants her to get married to a handsome man and he thinks that the handsome man is he himself."

Hearing this again there was a loud laughter. So Arti asked me that what was expected of her.

I said, "Can you please start talking to Rinki again. We would like to know what she thinks of Pappi. If Rinki still likes Pappi, then Pappi can approach her once more." Arti agreed to that.

The same day in evening Arti met Rinki at her home. Arti realized that although Rinki was laughing but there was something wrong. Arti asked her, "Rinki is there anything you are hiding behind your smile?"

Rinki said, "No everything's ok."

"I know there is something that you are hiding. Tell me are you happy with the person you are getting married?" Rinki was quiet at this.

After several seconds she broke her silence and said, "My father is forcing me to get married to a person who is a lot older than me just because he is a rich man and is settled in Dubai. The problem is I can't say no to my parents."

Arti asked, "I heard from someone that Pappi had proposed you once. I met one of his friends and he told me that he still loves you and will always wait for you."

Rinki burst out in tears and said, "Arti that was the biggest blunder that I have ever done in my life. I didn't know that Pappi loved me so much but you know that my brother and my father are so narrow minded. To be honest whenever he looked at me I saw the feeling of love in his eyes. I know he loves me but I cannot go against my parents."

Arti told us about whatever she had learnt from Rinki. Pappi was on cloud number nine.

I asked Arti to continue meeting Rinki and always talk about Pappi so that Rinki develops a strong liking for Pappi and she feels sorry for what she did to him. Arti did the same thing and she kept us informed regularly about the progress.

Rinki said to Arti one day that she is not able to forget the innocent face of Pappi when he proposed her. She spends sleepless nights and she wants to say sorry to Pappi. If only she meets him somewhere sometime.

Arti told this to us and Pappi was so happy that he jumped in joy yelling "Yeeeeaaaaaaaaaaahhhhhhhh".He thanked Arti for all the efforts she had given. I told him that now we are very close to our objective we need to arrange a meeting with Rinki.

I said to Pappi, "Listen you bugger. You will only have one chance to conquer Rinki's heart. Listen carefully if you want to have your love and lifc back you have to hit the bulls eye and that too in just one shot, so asshole you better prepare yourself."

Later that night Pappi couldn't sleep it felt to him as if there was some kind of fairy tale story going on where a Prince conquers the heart of a princess and takes her away in his golden chariot and they live happily ever after.

The third day in evening Arti came to the same park with Rinki. Pappi was very happy but at the same time was very nervous. I kept calming him down. Pappi asked me, "What will I say?"

"Tell her to go and marry that Dubai uncle. You idiot! Just go and open your heart in front of her."

We saw Arti and Rinki coming towards us. Rinki looked at Pappi and Pappi looked at her. Their eyes were fixed on each other. Time froze for both of them. Arti and I left that place for some time so that they could speak to each other and sort their lives out. They both walked close to each other. As they came near to each other Rinki's looked down and said in a lovely gentle voice, "Pappi don't stare at me like this."

Pappi said, "Why shouldn't I look at you, you are the most beautiful girl in this world I have ever seen in my life and I would like to keep staring at your beautiful face for the rest of my life. Can you please look into my eyes? Look into my eyes you will see what you mean to me."

Hesitantly she looked at him and said, "I hurt you Pappi. I can't even say sorry to you for what I did at that time."

"A man never gets hurt by the one he loves from the depth of his heart. So please don't feel bad. Just remember one thing that I love you and will love you forever. I have waited for you for so many years and will wait for you for the rest of my life. It's your decision, but to love you is my decision and I will stick to it. I have never ever put any condition in front of you that I love you so you will also have to love me. I'm making no plea to you to love me. In love there should be no condition or pleas or else the purity of love gets contaminated and I won't let anything to pollute the love which I have for you. I will love you always."

They sat on a bench and neither of them said anything. Silence ruled those several moments, but even in that silence love was connecting one heart to the other. A lot was being said and a lot was being heard. After several minutes Pappi heard a weeping sound and looked at Rinki she was crying. Damn Pappi! He wasn't carrying a handkerchief with him.

Suddenly he tore off the pocket of his shirt and wiped off the tears. He said, "These are too precious. Please don't let them fall. I'll keep them with myself."

He folded the cloth and kept it in his palm. Rinki smiled at him. Pappi stood up and went down on his knees and proposed her for one more time.

"Will you be mine forever, will you marry me. I love you!!"

She stood up, made Pappi stand up and hugged her tightly and said, "Yes I will."

Both of them embraced each other.

Now it was time for me and Arti to come out from the hiding. Rinki was silent once again. Arti said, "What happened? At least now be happy yaar."

“What about my marriage that is fixed to that uncle from Dubai? My father has already fixed it.” Rinki was worried.

I said, “Rinki I know Pappi's parents very well; they will never create any problem as far as love marriage is concerned. But you need to tell honestly about the reaction your parents will show.”

“My father strictly believes in arranged marriage and that too within the same caste. My brother Monu he is very much possessive about me and he will definitely create trouble for us.” Rinki sounded really tensed.

“If you are determined to marry Pappi and you stick to it then we can have a registered marriage in court. I will arrange everything for it.” I assured her.

“But what if after that too everything doesn’t become normal and there are fights then.”

Rinki was right. Pappi and Rinki didn’t have a strong stand on that as Pappi had just completed his engineering and was yet to start a career.

Pappi said, “We can do one thing I have a junior named Rajkumar. He is from Sagar. I am his favourite senior and had done lot for him, he once told me that if you have any problem he will help me, his elder brother is a don there. I will ask him to stay at his home till the time everything gets back to normal.”

I said, "Ok you confirm with him once again it will be a kind of preparation for us."

"What about my parents should I inform them or not." Pappi asked.

"You can tell Harshit and Mintoo. Also tell them once we are done with the legal formalities in court they can go to your home and tell your parents about it and try to clam them down. If Monu goes furious about it then we have the whole of MACT will be standing with you." I reassured him.

So it was decided that Pappi weds Rinki on Wednesday. Two days later. With some contacts we were able to file in an application on a back date of around a month.

Two days later Rinki came to the registrar's office dressed like a bride with Arti. Pappi almost fainted seeing the most beautiful girl of his life dressed like a bride: his bride. They got married with Arti and me signing as witnesses. It was the most special day for Pappi.

Mintoo and Harshit were then informed and they informed it to Pappi's parents. They were shocked and furious. Mintoo and Harshit tried to clam down the situation. After some shouting and fury they calmed down. Rinki called at her home and informed them about the marriage. Her family went raging with anger.

Everything happened as expected. Monu and Rinki's father went to Pappi's house and took Police along with them to arrest Pappi. Pappi went to Sagar with Rinki. Rajkumar arranged for their stay. Rinki's family created a lot of problems and Monu even vowed to kill both of them along with Arti and me. I went to Pappi's house the next day. Monu and Rinki's father were already there. Monu's anger and fury knew no limits. He charged on me.

I stopped him and said, "Look dude, now that your sister is married, you can do nothing. So just calm down and if you create problems I guarantee that I'll make your life a hell in this city."

I was wearing the MACT t-shirt and blazer. I pointed out at the logo and said to Monu, "You see this. I hope you know the power of this in this city as well. So dude just clam down and lets talk. Don't even try and touch this family, Arti or me." Hearing this Rinki's father controlled Monu and they left. I spoke to Pappi's parents and ensured that they were cool about this whole issue.

The situation didn't seem to settle down even after few weeks. Now Pappi's father decided to interfere so he asked me about Pappi and Rinki. I told him that they were safe. He wanted to speak to the couple. I had Pappi's contact number and I dialled it for him. Pappi picked up the phone and I told him to speak to his Dad.

His father said, “Son this situation will not be ok and it will go worse if you don’t come back and say sorry to Sehgal family. Come with Rinki we all will go together. They will not accept you as their son-in-law that is the fact. But you need to come I’m tired of answering everyone and Police.”

Pappi said, “Papa I don’t want to trouble you. Can you please give the phone to Anupam?” Uncle handed the phone to me.

I said, “Pups you come back with Rinki. I assure you everything will be fine and we will set everything alright.”

Pappi thanked Rajkumar for all the help he and his brother did to Pappi. The couple touched his parents feet took blessings and along with three other guys came back to Bhopal because it was risky to go alone to Bhopal.

Pappi’s mother was eager to see her ‘Bahu’ and son. She did all the possible decorations that was possible in short time and did a small puja for Pappi and Rinki. She was very happy to get a good ‘Bahu’ like Rinki. Everyone in Pappi’s home was happy. The only problem was with the Sehgal family.

Pappi’s father took the couple to the Police station. There they proved that the marriage being conducted was completely legal and within the government of India rules and regulations. Once the cops were convinced they ensured that nobody touches the couple.

Pappi's father wanted to take Pappi and Rinki to Sehgal's. I suggested that it would be better if I, Harshit and Mintoo too accompany them.

Rinki's mom opened the door. She hugged her daughter as soon as she saw her. But Rinki's father and Monu were very angry. Monu took a sword and came running towards us. Harshit and I stopped him by holding his hands.

Pappi said, "I know we have done this without your permission but we were in love and this was the only option you would have never agreed to our marriage that's why we took this path. I'm sorry about all this but I'm not guilty and I promise that no one in this world can ever love Rinki as much as I do. I will give her every joy and happiness in life. My parents have accepted her as their daughter."

Pappi said to Rinki's father, "Uncle my parents don't have a daughter. Please let Rinki become their daughter."

Silence prevailed in the room. No one said anything. After several minutes Sehgal Uncle cried and Monu too. They said, "We forgive you. Take her with you she is all yours and we know you love her too much."

Rinki's mom prepared snacks and tea. Sehgal Uncle said to Pappi's father, "*Bhai sahab apni dosti rishtedaari mai badal gayi hai* (Our friendship has now converted into relationship), but Rinki is our youngest child and we would like to get her married from our house. Can we have a big celebration and make it an arranged marriage. Please do not refuse."

Pappi's father said, "Even I wanted to say the same thing that our relatives and friends all should join in the celebration."

Pappi said, "Uncle, Dad, I want to say something."

His father said, "Yes son, what it is?"

Pappi said, "I have just completed my engineering and if you wish to have an arranged marriage then please let me make a career of my own, so that when we do this grand marriage ceremony, I can take responsibility of Rinki with full financial independence. It may take 3 or 4 years, but I'm sure when we are around 25 years of age, I will be able to pull off a grand celebrated wedding. Till then Rinki would be my keepsake with you. Please take good care of her."

Everyone and especially Rinki was stunned to hear this. But they all thought of this as step taken in self respect and dignity and everyone appreciated it.

Few weeks later Pappi got a job and moved to Indore. This started his journey as a successful software engineer with the love of Rinki as his support.

The day he left Bhopal Rinki's eyes were brimming with tears, the tears were a mixed feeling of being away from her love and also the hope that her love would return one day as a successful gentleman to take her with him on the golden chariot.

20

Untitled Incidents

June 2009, Pune: Almost a year has passed when I started writing this book and on an e-greeting I sent to Abhishikta, I promised that someday I would dedicate an entire book to her as a token of my love and today that promise has materialised.

Lost in my thoughts I heard the song 'I have become comfortable numb' as my mobile rang; it was Pappi.

"Yes mate."

"Where are you?"

"Office"

"Okay I'll reach in 15 minutes." Click.

15 minutes later Pappi came and we headed for a drink. Pappi asked, "Where to mate?"

“Wherever you say”

“Some place where there is peace and no crowd.”

“My apartment”

“*Chalega*”

On the way we picked up four bottles of beer and a bottle of Vodka.

Upon reaching my apartment I asked him about his visit to Canada.

“It was fabulous mate. Work was good, office was good and people were good. Everything was excellent.” Pappi said with excitement.

“Good that you enjoyed the visit.”

“Yeah but the only thing which I missed was Rinki. I missed her a lot.”

“I understand. How is she?”

“Beautiful, gorgeous and adorable as ever.”

“Even after all these years her beauty still fascinates you, doesn’t it.”

“Yes it does and not only her beautiful face fascinates me, it’s her beautiful soul which makes me fall in love with her. Every time I talk to her, I feel like taking more care of her. Every time she walks with me, I feel like protecting her more.”

“You surely love her with all your heart.”

Pappi just smiled and said, "Have you heard from Abhishikta."

The mere mention of the name moistened my eyes. Pappi knew that and kept quit. After a long silence I said, "No."

Pappi said, "Every thing was perfectly fine between the two of you till your final year. All of a sudden what happened?"

"I don't know. It was the Diwali of 2003, when I last had good talks with her."

"Good talks?"

"I mean when I had a normal jolly talk with her, shared jokes laughed and had good time. I called her up to wish her. Of course from my approach she knew I loved her. I went around her home and saw her, smiles exchanged."

"What happened that ended the good talks?"

"One day I met Shekar and he asked me that did I want a glorious opportunity to have Abhishikta forever."

"But I thought you and her were already going good."

"Yes, but then who doesn't want to expedite the process of getting the girl of his dreams. If you get a chance to impress Rinki even today, will you not do it?" Pappi nodded in agreement.

"He took me to Suresh, his friend and Abhishikta's classmate where I was told about Chakram another of their classmates that he liked Abhishikta a lot and had even tried to propose her couple of times and Abhishikta is pissed off with him."

"Next what?"

"Shekar said that since Chakram is bothering Abhishikta, so I should get rid of Chakram. This will make her go head over heels for me. I asked him how to do that and he replied that since I was in MACT I had the power in the city to do that."

"Was he suggesting beating up Chakram?"

"Yes, he was."

"Oh that fuckre!"

"I flatly denied"

"Good"

"I made my concern clear to him that I might lose Abhishikta if all this goes wrong. He dismissed that by saying that Suresh was her best friend and he would make things clear and would also bring her more close to me."

"Whoaaa! Did you believe it."

"No."

"So what happened next?"

"Suresh mentioned that a few days ago he and Abhishikta had furious verbal war with Chakram and she was upset. She had even asked Suresh to take care of Chakram by any means."

"Was that the truth, the complete truth and nothing else?"

"I don't know, and Shekar was a very good friend, I had no reason to not to believe Shekar."

"What happened next?"

"I called Sharma and asked me what I wanted to do" Sharma was Monu Sharma, my best friend in MACT.

"You wanted to beat the hell out of Chakram." Pappi said firmly.

"The next day I went to MACT with Shekar. From there Sharma made a call to Chakram and asked him to come down to MACT, he refused. Shekar said that Abhishikta and Chakram go to a (Common Admission Test) (CAT) coaching class in the evening. So we decided to go there and take care of the matter. So in the evening I along with Shekar, Sharma, B.P a School friend of Sharma and two of my classmates Karun and Kamlesh went to the coaching. After the class got over and students started to come out, we looked and looked, but neither Shekar saw Chakram nor did I see Abhishikta."

"Hmmm"

"We started off back for Mata Mandir on the way we stopped at Bittan Market, B.P had some important work. There was some friend of B.P who was into some kind of desktop printing business. Outside the shop we met a couple of guys. One of them was Chakram."

"Wow, that was some co-incidence. Keep going."

"Shekar confirmed that he was the one. Sharma had got a call from home, so he left. B.P and I took Chakram to a corner and I told him that we called him from MACT and I wanted to have a chat with him about Abhishikta so he must come with us. His face went white as a bedsheet. In the meanwhile one of the friends of Chakram who was drunk completely came; Chakram told him that we were from MACT and wanted to abduct him and beat him. He was completely out of his mind, so the lion in him came out. He warned me that if I touched Chakram he would beat the hell out me. With so many of us there started a war of words there. And we heard a Doppler's effect of a Police siren."

"Don't tell me all this was happening in front of the Habibganj Police station."

"It was. And the time was 11.00 P.M in the night."

“You guys got balls man.”

“I asked Chakram for the last time whether he was coming with me or not. He denied. I got so pissed off with that I almost slapped him but B.P stopped me and made me realize that we were in front of a Police station and any kind of violence at this hour could prove fatal. So we left. The next morning I got a call from Sharma. He asked me to come to his place immediately and pick him up. I rushed to his place. He asked me to head straight for Abhishikta’s coaching. Now I could read his mind clearly. We reached, there I saw Abhishikta going inside the Classroom, but I couldn’t find Chakram. So we decided to wait.”

“Did he turn up?”

“Yes within a few minutes, he came with another guy both of them smoking. Seeing me he once again went pale. Sharma grabbed him by collar and dragged him to a corner. WHACK! WHACK! Two slaps on Chakram. He started crying and asked what he had done wrong. I told him everything.”

“Didn’t he deny all the charges put on him?”

“Yes he did, I called Shekar and made Chakram talk to him. When I spoke to Shekar he confirmed that I have done the right thing. By now the other guy with Chakram who was introduced to us as his senior, his name I can’t recall started to shout that it was wrong. The moment he uttered the words *'Sharma Bhai yeh tumne sahi nahi kiya'* (Sharma dude you this is wrong) WHACK! WHACK! He got two slaps from Sharma. He was shocked by that and was about to burst in tears and said that it was wrong; WHACK! I gave him a tight one and asked him to keep quiet."

"That was mind blowing?"

"I asked Chakram to keep away from Abhishikta or else I would dig up his grave in some corner of the huge seven hundred acre campus of MACT. WHACK! Sharma gave him one more blow and instructed to him to do exactly as I say."

"So did he follow your instructions?"

"What do you think?"

"Anyone except a fool or a mad man who wants to commit a suicide would have denied."

"He even got his CAT coaching class batch changed to a different batch."

"Wow!"

"After that we left and went to Bittan Market. There we went to the shop from which that drunken asshole came out, but fortunately for that asshoel the shop was closed being Sunday. We decided to have a smoke there and as we started with our NAVY CUTS a boy came. His pillion was the same senior of Chakram. As he got down from his bike he asked whether we were Anupam and Sharma. Sharma confirmed. The moment Sharma confirmed, he started hurling abuses in hindi starting with madarchod bhanchod Sharma said '*Bas oye, kaun hai tu?*' (Enough who are you?) To this he replied that he was Abhishikta's brother and accused me of chasing and hazing Abhishikta."

"What the fuck! Where did this brother asshole come from?" Pappi said in surprise.

"Even I wondered. I said Abhishikta doesn't have a brother where the fuck do you come from? He said that he was not his real brother, but he called her sister."

"What was his name?"

"He was some Nitiraj. He didn't look like a guy who would take a girl as beautiful as Abhishikta to be his sister and the way he was advocating Chakram and that our beating him was wrong, raised suspicions that why would a brother get bothered if someone like Chakram who is chasing his sister gets beaten up by someone, it didn't make sense. He said that next time he sees me within a radius of five kilometres of Abhishikta, he would kill me."

"Wow!"

"This fired up our anger but we kept calm. Sharma asked him what does he do and he replied that he has passed out from LNCT one of the private engineering colleges in Bhopal and he is preparing for CAT and goes to the same coaching where Abhishikta does."

"Now was this is co-incidence or anything else."

"I don't know. I wanted to be sure whatever he was saying was true or he was just making it up. So I asked him to make a call to Abhishikta and speak to her about it. I was quite sure that by now Shekar would have let Suresh know that Chakram had got a nice boot on his ass and this would have been communicated to Abhishikta in the right sense by now."

"So did Nitiraj make the call?"

"Well no, on the contrary what he said that because of some problems in Abhishikta's life he cannot call at her home. That rang a bell in my head, first what kind of problems would stop a brother from calling his sister. Second, neither of her close friends including Suresh knew that she was in so much of a deep trouble that even her brother couldn't call her. He even mentioned that he was also a friend of my senior from the Architecture branch of MACT Kirtesh sir. Sharma spoke to Kirtesh sir and we asked him to meet us that evening at MACT square in the evening to discuss the matter."

"So what happened next?"

"That afternoon the asshole called me. He said sorry at least a zillion times for the abuses. That clicked my head that why does a brother of a sister have to say sorry in such matters. I asked him to meet in the evening and we can talk then. After that I immediately dialled Sharma. He said that he too got a call from the asshole and he too asked him to meet in the evening. Evening came I went to pick up Sharma. There I found Nilesh there another of my best buddy. We went straight to the Hostel number 5 of MACT, called up Karun and Kamlesh. All five of us reached MACT square. After a while Nitiraj turned up, we greeted him."

"You greeted him!"

"Yes dude we greeted him offered him smoke, coz I needed to know what the truth was. Truth that probably never reached Abhishikta."

"I see."

"He asked about Kirtesh sir and Sharma said that he would come to Mata Mandir so lets go there. Upon reaching there we didn't find Kirtesh sir there. We started talking and after some time the truth started to come out."

"So what was the exciting news?"

"The news was that Mr. Asshole aka Nitiraj was no brother of Abhishikta, in fact as he attended the same CAT coaching class. At the beginning of classes when Nitiraj saw Abhishikta for the first time, he too fell in true love with her, but later Chakram fell in love with Abhishikta and so he sacrificed his true love for him and the reason, he sacrificed his so-called love for Abhishikta was because that senior of Chakram was a friend of Nitiraj and he asked him to get out of the way of Chakram and Abhishikta"

"And did Abhishikta know that?"

"You are talking about Nitiraj falling in infatuation with her."

Pappi nodded.

"No. By this time night had fallen and it was almost 10.00pm and Kirtesh sir hadn't turned up. Sharma went to get a few NAVY Cuts, but I knew there was something else in his mind."

"What?"

"He went to call Kirtesh sir. He came back lighted the cigarette and said, "Bhosdike, now what should we do with you?" these words came like a jolt to his ears. He was wondering how could someone who was so friendly only 5 minutes ago turn so violent. WHACK! WHACK! WHACK! WHACK! WHACK! Came five tight slaps from Sharma and also the words "Never ever take a MACTian for granted" Nitiraj said sorry. WHACK! From Karun "Bohosdike never try to play around with a MACTian" WHACK! WHACK! Came two sound punches from Kamlesh "Sun harami

MACTians don't tolerate sorries." WHACK! A blow from Nilesh "MACTians don't compromise, if you have made a mistake with a MACTian, you have to repay for it." WHACK! It was my blow and with that he landed on the ground weeping hard and as he fell he took the brunt of my kicks. His upper lip got a big cut, bleeding like hell. Kamlesh, Karun and Nilesh started to kick with the most severity that they could. After few minutes Karun and Kamlesh were stopped by Sharma. Nitiraj was helped to stand up on his legs."

"Okay, so what happened next?"

"He said that if Kirtesh sir would have been here we couldn't have even touched him, he was crying like hell. To this Sharma said, "What do you think, why Kirtesh sir hasn't turned up even after 3 hours of wait at Mata Mandir? He knew what had to happen to you'."

"So what happened next?"

"We gave him some water and then let him go. The next day I met Kirtesh sir and he said, last night Nitiraj after being thrashed came directly to him and he cried and puked."

"Puked? Why?"

"I don't know."

"Was he mad at you guys for hitting his friend?"

"Yes, he said, you idiots, why did you leave him alive, you should have killed that son of a bitch."

"Wow! What happened next?"

"That's the question I had been trying to find an answer to. After this incident everything seemed like settling down. I called Abhishikta a few times, but couldn't talk to her as she would not be at home. I got busy with my projects and research work which I was doing for various national and international organisations and the deadlines for the submission of research reports were closing in fast. But Suresh and Shekar told me that the whole episode has been narrated to Abhishikta in a very good sense and she is feeling good that I helped her."

"Okay so when the things did actually went wrong."

"I don't know exactly, but to me it was the trivial day of 7th of January 2004."

"Your Birthday!"

"Yeah my birthday, I wanted to talk to Abhishikta desperately and propose her. I called her. Her sister picked up the phone. I asked for Abhishikta, she asked me to hold on. Abhishikta came and her sister said 'Anupam' and click! She simply disconnected the line."

"What the fuck was that? Why didn't she talk to you, she was talking to you sweetly almost a month and a half ago what happened? You two were going on the right track of made for each other."

"I dialled her number again; all I wanted to say was that it was my birthday and I wanted tell her I loved her with all my heart and soul. The phone rang, Abhishikta picked up the call and said 'Hello' once again that sweet voice made me fall in love with her head over heels. As I said Hello, she asked "Who is this?" I said Anupam and the hell broke down on me, she said, "Enough! The next time you call me or bother me I'm going to complain it to the Police and throw you behind bars. Never ever call me again!" Click! She hung up. I felt like being struck by schizophrenia, my mind went out of order. Disturbed and wrecked completely. I couldn't figure out what was going on wrong. I was not even given the chance to ask what I did wrong. I collapsed on my bed and tears started flowing out, I cried and cried and cried."

"fuck man, why didn't she even give you a chance to say a word after 'Hello'. What does she think of herself? I feel pity for Abhishikta; she disregarded and dismissed the boy who loved her most on this planet and you call her the most matured girl you have ever seen or met; bloody hell."

"After several minutes the phone rang again I looked at the phone hoping it would be Abhishikta feeling sorry for yelling at me on my birthday, I picked up the phone, it was Sharma. He asked where are we celebrating today, I just said to him that I don't want to celebrate. He sensed something terrible has happened. He asked me to come down to his place. With shaky legs I got up and set off, thinking what went wrong? I did not have a way to find out answers to these questions. Like a robot I took the route which led me to Abhishikta's home. As I crossed, I looked and found nothing but darkness. I stopped in front of her house and stared at the complete darkness. After that I went to Sharma there B.P and Nilesh were present already. Sharma came out and hopped on my bike and then said lets go. We went to a dhaba and there Sharma asked me what happened. I narrated every single detail to him. He immediately took out his cell phone and called Shekar. He told him everything that happened to me that evening, also told him that I was crying. He asked Shekar to come to the dhaba immediately. But Shekar he never came to the dhaba we waited till 1.00am but he never came instead he switched off his mobile phone and asked his family to tell any caller that he is not at home."

"What! You joking, that asshole did that."

"No jokes, it's my life, yes he did."

"Bloody son of a bitch"

"Yeah bloody son of a bitch and since that day he has never shown his face to me."

"Hmmm I see, it was only after that Shekar and Suresh persuaded you to beat Chakram for some of their unnamed benefits. They used Abhishikta for that reason and later on apparently it seems that some other story was telecasted to Abhishikta which brings a bad name to Abhishikta because of you and which made her furious on you."

"Yes it seems like this, but I could never ever get hold of Shekar or Suresh to know their deeds. Even today if I find that fucking son of a bitch,

By all means he's gonna die, doesn't matter what happens to me later on but that asshole

is going to die, I just need some favourable conditions and he is dead."

"So did you not try to contact Abhishikta ever after that?"

"Tried? Damn I gave in everything to contact her; e-mails, chat, greeting cards and what not, but she never responded back."

"That was all?"

"Yeah that was all."

"When was the last time you saw her?"

"Last year Mumbai. Before leaving for Manchester. I heard that she was in Mumbai, so I went there and managed to get a glimpse of her."

"Now you just keep remembering her even without getting a chance to ever see her face even once."

"I still remember her face and she still has that innocence and aura in her face, which she had ten years ago. I have that photograph of her, so I can see her whenever I want to."

"Bloody hell. What the fuck? She made your life a mess and you let her do that."

"Yes because I love her, I love her as much as you love Rinki, didn't she make your life a mess few years ago, and you let her do that."

"I know but I can't see you just crying all the way for Abhishikta, just ruining you life for someone who doesn't even care."

"I'm not crying buddy, I love her and I'm waiting for her, it's a part of my love to keep loving her for the rest of my life, unconditionally and with the utmost purity of soul, even though luck and fate has made me an untouchable not even worthy of having a glimpse of the Goddess he loves and worships. But if that is the price I pay for loving Abhishikta, I'm ready to pay it not just for this life, but even for the life after this and after that and after that and forever."

Epilogue:

Two weeks later when I came home I was happy and tired. Tired, because I came back from the airport; was bugged down by the crowd and the delayed flights. No it wasn't me who was travelling. I came back after seeing off Pappi and Rinki for their honeymoon in Singapore.

That night I just felt very happy for Pappi, at least he got the title of his life and his life no longer remained UNTITLED. But for me, I sat under the cover of darkness with tears in my eyes and my mind wandering in my past, the past which was made of Abhishikta, past which had love for Abhishikta in form of smiles and lovely talks. The tears in my eyes were my present, which had love for Abhishikta, but that love which I had lost; lost forever, she had so much hate for me in her heart that she would never understand my love, my actions whatever they were but were only because I loved her and now she would never come in my arms and say 'Anupam I Love You and I'm here to make your life beautiful.' But to me my love for her was a never ending one; I would love her till perpetuity and would wait for her till one day in one of my birth when she would come and say those three magical words to me. And it's not my wish, it's my determination and I will wait in every birth for that to happen. I couldn't control the tears in my eyes, the feeling was so tumultuous for me that I left my apartment with the only love I had left in my life my bike and zoomed off into the darkness not knowing where I was heading to but with Abhishikta in my heart, my mind kept saying 'I Love You Abhishikta, I Love You Abhishikta'; and with my life still UNTITLED.